NEVER M

"You *want* me to curse you?" I asked Bart, loving the fear in his eyes. "Is that why you're provoking me?" His cockiness was disappearing fast, now. "I keep telling you guys over and over, when you mess with me and mine, it's gonna start raining curses."

"Whatever," he said, trying to look bored, but backing off. It always kills me how the tough ones are fastest to crumble. Bart was no exception. "Listen, we were just—"

He flinched when I moved toward him, already muttering my spell. When I reached the ash can, I leaned down and grabbed two handfuls of ashes and butts—and there was plenty to grab. I stuck out my left arm and rubbed one handful of grimy mess over the inside. Then I repeated the gesture with the right. I let the powder fall to the ground and thrust out my arms so everyone could see.

YOU'RE DEAD MEAT, said my right arm in the magical letters that the ashes had left behind. The other arm had the same creepy letters spelling out his name: BART NELSON!

YOU ARE *SO* CURSED!

NAOMI NASH

SMOOCH NEW YORK CITY

SMOOCH ®

March 2004

Published by

Dorchester Publishing Co., Inc.
200 Madison Avenue
New York, NY 10016

ISBN 0-8439-5310-1

The name "SMOOCH" and its logo are trademarks of Dorchester
Publishing Co., Inc.

Printed in the United States of America.

Visit us on the web at www.smoochya.com.

ACKNOWLEDGMENTS

Every conjuror needs an assistant—I've been blessed with several. I owe many thanks to Andrew Wright, Tahirah Shadforth, Jonathan Logan, and Terry Danuser for their helpful suggestions and support; and to my editor, Kate Seaver, and my agent, Michelle Grajkowski, for their never-flagging encouragement. I'm deeply indebted to Patty Woodwell for her proofreading and continuity skills, and especially to Marthe Arends, the finest critique partner a writer could ever have. Most of all, I thank my husband for making every day magical.

CHICAGO PUBLIC LIBRARY

TEEN

VOLUME

Teen Volume is made possible
by a grant from the
McCormick Tribune Foundation
through the Chicago Public Library Foundation

McCormick
Tribune
Foundation

Chapter One

"You know what your problem is, Marotti? You've got attitude. You think you're better than the rest of the school. Listen up. I've got your number, and you're not so tough!"

My first thought, nose-to-nose with Vice Principal Dermot, was that he really needed to floss more often. Even yearly would be a start. Trust me—a man who swills down cafeteria fish sticks with main office coffee ends up with breath that could give rotten eggs a run for their money. But what could I do? He had me pinned up against the principal's door, where he'd been lurking outside, waiting to pounce. My upper lip curled to keep his breath from toasting my nose hairs.

"See what I mean? Attitude. It won't win you friends, and that'll be your downfall, young lady."

Dermot looked at me like the diaper filled with steaming goat poo that the football team left last year on his desk as a prank. I could tell what he thought as he looked me over. *Hair that's darker than natural. Lipstick three shades more sinister than it should be. Black nail polish, black clothes, too much kohl. Scourge of the sophomore class.* Every little vein in his eyes throbbed with a single word: *Freak!*

You know, any other kid in this school could hawk nuclear weapons and illegal diet pills right on the school's front steps and never have to see the inside of Mac-Alister's office. The Doormat came down on me if I so much as crossed my eyes. Before he could blast me again with the Flipper breath, I smiled and turned on the charm. "Gee, Dermot, it's been *real* swell, but Principal Mac-Alister told me to get right back to my class, and I'd *hate* her to think I wasn't a team player, you know?" I swung under his sweat-stained armpit and began my trek down the hall. It's not my fault he had slow reflexes, right?

"Vice *Principal* Dermot, young lady!" Potato, potahto. Honestly, you'd think the guy would have something better to do than stand around and get his thong in a twist about a stupid job title. "You might think you're better than everyone else in this school, but I assure you, Victoria Marotti, that you are not better than *me!*"

See ya! Wouldn't want to be ya! I thought, letting the Doormat say good-bye to my backside.

The people in this miserable pit are so ignorant. Take Principal MacAlister, with her little lectures on how we're all in one great big boat together and the ship can't pull away from shore until everyone grabs an oar. Whatever! And I don't know how Dumpster-breath Doormat could ever think I had delusions of superiority.

Me, better than anyone in the Hair Club for Harpies, with their pretty faces and pretty makeup and pretty little Barbie outfits pressed perfectly for their pretty yearbook photos? Better than the grinds, always ready with their homework and their hands in the air, the geeks the teachers adored? Better than the jocks everyone worshiped, and the skateboard guys who were the class clowns, and the band kids in their new uniforms? Hardly!

Boy, oh, boy, though, did they ever scatter whenever I strutted down the hallway. I always enjoyed that part of my social exile. One kid was in such a hurry to run from me that he stumbled and fell against the locker. Part of me instinctively wanted to say, "Oops! Let me help!" Instead, I turned my head away and let the strings from my sweatshirt hood swing back and forth as I kept walking. Dermot was right about one thing: I had attitude to spare.

What most people don't understand is that attitude is about the easiest thing in the world to fake. You jut out your jaw. You stare. You pretend you're not paying attention and that you don't care. Real soon, everyone begins buying it. People never look further than your exterior, anyway. They think the pretty-pretty people are just as beautiful inside. Me? I liked people to think that I was tough—that I was dangerous. My outside was a warning to anyone who looked my way: *I'm not going to be your victim*.

Two of the Hair Club girls, both of them wearing little pink outfits apparently plucked from the skimpier racks of Slutbombs-R-Us, blocked my path to the lunchroom.

3

Melinda Scott and DeMadison Cook. Oh, peachy—the yearbook treasurer and one of her flunkies. I knocked against Melinda with my shoulder, merely because she was in my way. "Hey!" she whined. Her complaint vanished when she saw who'd bumped her.

I turned around, raised my eyebrows, and held my hands out to the sides. I learned the move from a movie. "You want a piece of this?" the guy in it kept threatening. "You want a piece of *this?*" Only I kept quiet.

Although I'd performed this tough act for a year, I still felt a moment of doubt every single time I hardened my heart and slapped on the sneer. Were they going to call my bluff? Were they going to guess what a marshmallow I really was? Melinda fell for it, though. She and DeMadison shut their glossy little lips, backed off, and didn't say anything until I wheeled around again. "Witch," I heard DeMadison mutter, but I could afford to pretend I didn't. Would my picture make it into the yearbook next to Melinda and her photogenic little chums? Doubtful. Socially, I was the Limburger cheese on a buffet table full of Kraft slices. No one said boo to my face, though—that was the trade-off I'd made, and I accepted it.

I hated the cafeteria. Add together the geeks with food in their braces, the Hair Club girls and their diets, the food throwers, the practical jokers, and the hair nets on the workers, and you've got a supreme-court argument for abolishing high school as a cruel and unusual punishment. My usual table was the worst in the room. It lurked in the very back corner, under the dripping window where no one wants to sit. Something about it seemed

4

a bit off, though. One hundred noisy tables full of kids yelling, and then one tiny table with two friends of mine who looked like they were about to take their SATs hung upside down over a pit of hungry alligators. It was like one of those "which of these things is not like the others?" puzzles.

"You guys look freaked," I told them. "Where's Addy? Where's Ray?"

Neither wanted to tell me. "Des? Is something wrong?" Desiree had a habit of gnawing on her lips and fingers when she was miserable, which was most of the time. She avoided my question by looking down at the table. The skin around her mouth was already so red and scabbed; I was happy to see Dorie nudge her to stop. "Hello? Like, this year, guys?"

Avoidance was contagious, apparently. Dorie hid her face behind a copy of *Dreemboyz* magazine. Apparently she had decided any further questions should be directed to the smiling boy band S.W.A.K.

"Lost sight of Addy. It's like she vanished out there." Ray, another member of our little losers' club, walked up with crossed arms. Usually it's hard to tell when Ray's agitated, but he so rarely spoke two sentences in a row that I clued in immediately. "Uh-oh," he said, noticing me for the first time.

"Out where?" I growled. Protecting these kids was my daily job, and evasion wasn't helping me get the job done.

Dorie lifted her face from the green glop in her bowl. "Pop Alley."

5

"Is she in trouble?"

Des looked at Dorie. Dorie looked at Ray. Ray looked at the ceiling. "I don't know if I'd call it trouble, exactly."

I said a swear word. Actually, it was the same swear word that had landed me in Principal MacAlister's office, which is the same swear word that even my grandmother in Cleveland says when she loses at bingo, but for some reason it's supposed to have eluded my vocabulary. "I keep telling you guys never to go out to Pop Alley alone!"

It was no use crabbing at them, though. They're scared of everyone, like I used to be. Addy was like that, too. In fact, I was surprised she'd ventured off on her own. Now I had to find her before trouble beat me to it.

I'd already pulled one of my arms into my sweatshirt when I turned and slammed into someone. It wasn't deliberate that time. In my old marshmallow days I would have cowered and apologized at the mistake. Not now, though. "Real graceful, roadkill!" I snarled.

Roadkill turned around. I'd seen him once or twice, but didn't know him. I don't usually pay a lot of attention to the guys in my school. He was kind of blond, kind of brown-eyed, kind of a square jaw, more than kind of attractive. The enemy, in other words. I cocked my head, not planning to waste a lot of time on the confrontation.

When guys at school grin at me, it's usually a prelude to some sad attempt to mock me. "Sorry," he said.

"Whatever." I brushed by with my hand held up in warning. I didn't need his kind making fun of me. I had Addy to find.

Pop Alley is a sidewalk running from the cafeteria exit

to the teachers' parking lot. A huge corrugated metal roof slants over a bunch of vending machines lined up against the building. The reek of old tobacco hit me like a baseball bat. I reeled back, knowing I'd have to dump my clothes in the wash the second I got home. Well, the sweatshirt was coming off anyway. "Addy?" I called out.

"Vick?" My head snapped in the direction of the last of the soda machines. Pinned to its far side was Addy, my best friend. I saw her lunch box first, followed by her frizzy red hair. Addy was probably the only high school student in the entire world who brought sandwiches in a Hello Kitty lunch box. Not because Hello Kitty was trendy, but because she thought Hello Kitty was cute.

Addy's face was flushed when she craned to see me. "Oh, jeez, it's Marotti," said the guy hovering over her. He pushed himself upright, but kept Addy pinned between his arms. Then he said the very same swear word I'd used seconds before, the one that none of us are supposed to know.

"Nelson." I used his same snide tone, angry but trying to sound cool. I'd already pulled my other arm into my sweatshirt when I stepped outdoors; I drew it over my head and tossed it on the ground and then tugged down my tank top. Addy's flush deepened. To her I probably looked like Wonder Woman and Charlie's Angels to the rescue, all rolled up in one. "New toy, Nelson? What's the matter, get bored with your Easy-Bake oven?"

He gave me a steely look. Smoke poured out between his lips as he stubbed out his cigarette on top of the stone ash can. Addy sidled past him and ran behind me once

7

he moved. "I'm all right," she told me. "Really!"

"Yeah, it's cool. We were just talking."

"Oh, really?" I cracked my fingers. Like I said, it's not that hard to look tough. Bart Nelson seemed to have it down pat, but I was the expert. You pretend the world's yours. Ignoring other people's personal space helps, too. I drew myself up as tall as possible and squared off against him. "Talking about what? The fine arts? The cinema? What Beetle Bailey said to Sarge this morning?"

I'd seen that stupid grin spreading across his lips before. Bart wore it in class when he thought he was getting away with murder. I hated that grin. While I mentally plotted out my approach, a crowd gathered around us, some of them spilling out from the cafeteria. Fine with me. I liked an audience for my performances.

"Wouldn't you like to know?" He looked me up and down, practically licking his chops like Wile E. Coyote being served a Roadrunner TV dinner. "You know, Marotti, you'd be pretty hot yourself, if you weren't such a—"

My philosophy? When they've got a one-track mind, boys deserve what's coming to them. With all my strength I swung both my hands up toward his face as if I intended to catch him in a double punch. He snapped back as I crossed them at the wrists in the space between our faces. "Such a what?" I asked him, real sweetly. "If I weren't such a witch?"

The dozen kids behind me got real quiet all of a sudden. I heard Addy plead, "Vick, don't do this!"

"You *want* me to curse you?" I asked Bart, loving the fear in his eyes. "Is that why you're provoking me?" His cockiness was disappearing fast now. "I keep telling you guys over and over, when you mess with me and mine, it's gonna start raining curses."

"Whatever," he said, trying to look bored, but backing off. It always kills me how the tough ones are the fastest to crumble. Bart was no exception. "Listen, we were just—"

He flinched when I moved toward him, already muttering my spell. When I reached the ash can, I leaned down and grabbed two handfuls of ashes and butts— and there was plenty to grab. I stuck out my left arm and rubbed one handful of grimy mess over the inside. Then I repeated the gesture with the right. I let the powder fall to the ground and thrust out my arms so everyone could see.

YOU'RE DEAD MEAT, said my right arm in the magical letters that the ashes had left behind. The other arm had the same creepy letters spelling out his name: BART NELSON! The black soot against my skin made the curse seem doubly toxic.

Again I had that moment of doubt. Would Bart see through me? I watched his lips move as he read the message. "That's freakin' impossible," he stammered.

"Is it?" I challenged him. "Huh. Survey says . . . you're toast!"

He said that swear word again, my grandmother's favorite, and added to it a whole bunch more that should've landed him in MacAlister's office for life. I sprang in his direction like I was going to attack him. His reflexes made him turn and run like the chicken he was.

"Anyone else want some? Anybody?" I asked the crowd. All the gawkers pretended they weren't looking. In fact, they all acted as if they suddenly had to be somewhere else. "Freak," I heard one of them say to another.

Well, yeah. I might be a freak. What's important to me, though, is that people think Vick Marotti is the kind of freak you don't mess with.

Within thirty seconds only two people were left under the shelter of Pop Alley. Addy I'd expected to stay. The one I didn't figure on was Roadkill, the guy I'd bumped into earlier. Tall, blond, and pretty boy. He studied me like I was some kind of problem he'd been assigned to puzzle out. I was all ready to slice and dice him when all of a sudden he started laughing. Laughing! At me! He grinned and clapped like I was the featured performer of *Voodoo on Ice!*, gave me the thumbs-up, and sauntered off back to the cafeteria. Talk about freaks!

"Who is *he?*" I asked Addy.

"I was getting a soda pop," she protested, still flustered. "I wish you wouldn't always come running after me."

"You know better than to come out here by yourself during lunch, with all the losers that hang here," I scolded. "Man, some days I really have to work my butt off to protect you guys from yourselves!"

She tucked some of her frizzies behind her ears. "You're always telling us we need to stand up for ourselves. You complain about having to shelter us, then you complain when we take a risk. You can't have it both ways!"

"I've saved you from being pushed around more times than I can count!"

She softened at the reminder. "I know. I know. It's just . . . usually I'm really glad my best friend is a witch." She put her arms around my neck to give me a quick hug. "But not today."

Addy was the first person at Fillmore to show me any kindness when I transferred schools last year. Not a single day passed that I didn't think I was the worst friend possible for her. She had no idea that the one thing I most wanted to tell her was the one thing I never, ever could.

You see, I wasn't a witch at all.

CHAPTER TWO ⊙

Sometimes I wonder why moms and dads bother giving kids names. By the time we're in high school, we're all supermarket bargain brands with generic titles: *Corn Flakes. Puffed Rice.* Instead of cereals, though, here you can walk through the halls and pick out *Tattooed Boy* and *Girl Whose Dad Bought Her an SUV*.

If you're unlucky, like most of my friends, you get the names that hurt. Like *Midget* or *Scabby* or *Fat Girl*. Ray was *That Girl Who Pretends She's a Guy*. Today he was wearing an oversize football shirt and jeans hung low around his hips. A bright yellow baseball cap sat backward on his head. Yeah, so underneath all Ray's clothes and mannerisms were girl parts. I still don't get the fuss. Why the name-calling and the pushing around? I mean, if you hit the DQ for something good 'n' frosty and you don't like the strawberry dip, don't *get* the strawberry dip. Don't beat up the rest of us for not getting a vanilla cone like yours!

Addy followed Ray to the spot where I sat alone, as always, on a bench at the edge of the school grounds. The sun made my eyes water when I looked up. "Hey, guys."

"Ray knows something about him."

"About who?"

"Roadkill."

Ray stood with his arms crossed, eyes half-closed, looking to all the world as if his name were Toughie Mc-Biteme. He'd been letting his upper lip fuzz grow, and accented it with a little eyeliner. Of all the kids in my little losers' club, Ray had learned the most about looking like you take nothing from nobody. "Yo." He sounded gruff and distant.

"Yo," I said back. " 'Sup, dawg?"

Ray gave me a long, steady look like I'd been fresh-picked out of the stupid patch. "Yo, not *yo*. Joe."

"Joe?"

"G-I-O. *Gio.*"

Addy stopped chewing her braid and broke in. "Roadkill's name is Gio. He's in Ray's AP English class."

"Yeah." Ray has won poetry contests and had once been asked to read one of his poems at the dedication of the new City Hall. Only at Fillmore can someone be so talented, and yet still be Alpo at the social buffet. "Gio Carson. He's pretty cool."

"What do you mean, pretty cool? I thought you hated the kids in that class." Ray shrugged. I could tell this wasn't getting us anywhere. "So what is he? Jock? Geek? Gay? Netzoid? Nerd?" I ran through the list.

"Band boy? Choir boy? Fundie? Rich kid, club kid, beggar kid, thief?"

Swear to God, if Ray shrugged one more time . . . but he did. Before I could shake his pants off, though, he actually spoke a few of the words with which he's allegedly so good. "He's not really part of a crowd. Gets along with everyone. Everyone likes Gio." It was with a slight smile that he looked off at the school and mumbled, " 'S never called me a freak or anything. He's pretty cool."

Hmmmm. Interesting.

"Are you into him or something?" Addy asked me.

I gave her a look of scorn. Into him? Hardly! "Whatcha got there?" I pretended the subject was closed and grabbed a little bundle of notebook paper from her hand.

We'd been through this routine dozens of times. "Notes for my big history paper— Oh, Vick, please don't . . . !" I danced away from her. She winced as I passed off the pages behind my back from hand to hand. Right in front of her face, i shredded them into a hundred bits.

Addy sighed and rolled her eyes. "Say the spell and bring it back, already. *Please.* It's my big history project and if I don't . . ."

I was already three steps ahead of her, of course. I bundled up all the paper bits into a ball, popped them into my mouth, and then pulled her notes, magically whole again, from my sweatshirt.

" . . . half my entire *grade* and . . . Oh, thank you." She took the notes back and tucked them away in her knapsack. "I'm glad you used a dry spell. It was gross that time you regurgitated my French homework."

"I wish you knew witchcraft that *did* my trig assignments for me," Ray said with a note of sorrow.

Mission accomplished. By the time I departed for the bus stop, they'd both forgotten all conversation about that boy from yesterday.

So. Roadkill had a name, did he? Gio. Everybody liked Gio. Oh, that was ripe. How was school today, Gio? How's Mama's little boy, Gio? Need a ride to school? Sure, I'll give you a lift in my Gio. You don't mind that Mommy and Daddy couldn't find you a real name, do you, Gio? Could your hair be any more perfect, Gio? Gio, Gio, wherefore art thou, Gio?

"Hello!" Who was talking to me? I turned. Holy eye of newt! It was Gio. What the heck? Was he following me? Panicked as I felt, some little part of my brain instructed me to turn around and ignore him. My body paid about as much attention to that little part of my brain as my brain pays attention to the nutritional information on a bag of Doritos when I'm on a junk-food binge. I stood there and looked at him, because the looking was so, so tasty.

"Hello?" He sounded unsure I'd heard him the first time. In normal conversation it would have been up to me to say something. The mere thought of replying made me want to flop sweat.

"Blurgh!" Swear to God, I meant to say, "Paint yourself a picture, Picasso," but that's how it came out.

"Umm." Crapola. He thought I was a total freak! Okay, I'm used to people thinking I'm a total freak, but I like them to think I'm a dangerous, possibly homicidal freak who'd rip out their tongue if they said the wrong thing. I couldn't bear his thinking I'm the kind of freak who might giggle, vomit on his shoes, and be carted off to the funny farm by the nice doctors bringing the big white jacket with the extra-long arms.

"I'm great," I said, forcing myself to speak that language I once knew. English, I think it was called. "I'm fantastic. Wait, you asked how I was, right?" Hadn't he? He grinned at me and blinked, obviously confused but enjoying himself. "Listen, Roadkill, I'm fine. You should try me sometime."

You should try me sometime? Where in the world did *that* come from? I sounded like some kind of cheap, easy . . . when I was just the opposite!

If he noticed my little slip of the tongue, he didn't let on. Good. Maybe he hadn't heard. "I was wondering if we could have a talk?" he said.

"I don't think so." Looking at the road was easier than looking at that pretty square jaw and spiky hair.

"Aw, come on. It's easy."

The way he spoke to me, like I was one of his actual acquaintances, unnerved me. He obviously wanted something from me. "No, it's not."

"It's easy in my world!"

"Well, in *my* virgin, this conversation isn't even . . ." *Virgin*. Oh, God. Oh, good God. Had I used the word *virgin* for *version?* I blinked several times. He had already raised his eyebrows, surprised at me. Maybe there was a way I could recover? Maybe? No?

The silence between us grew longer and longer while

I stood paralyzed with panic. I couldn't think of a thing to say. This conversation was going to be all over school the next morning, I knew. Virgin jokes everywhere. Crapola! Just as I was about to fall to my knees and beg a sinkhole to open up and suck me under, I heard the roar of a diesel engine and felt a rush of air at my back. The city bus opened its door. Escape!

"Hey! I wanted to talk to you!" he shouted after me. Too late! I hauled butt past an old lady burdened with shopping bags so I could be first on that bus. Until Gio's blond hair was only a shiny little speck from the bus's back window, I didn't dare breathe.

All the rest of that day, my slip of the tongue bugged me. I mean, I don't even *notice* boys. It's not that I don't like them—I'm not that way. See, I divide my goals into the short-term and the long-term. My short-term goal is to get me and my friends through the school day without any of us getting beaten up. My long-term goal? To endure the four-year-long root canal without Novocain, called high school. Boys would have to wait until after, when things were quieter and the people more real.

Wasn't dating overrated, anyway? I thought about it later that night as I got ready for bed. I mean, you go out, you mash your lips together, you try to Just Say No to the other stuff, you pick out some goopy pop dirge that gets overplayed on the radio and say it's your song, and then you act totally possessive of each other whenever you're both in the same room, effectively creeping out your friends. Who needs that?

I put away my pentacle earrings, climbed out of about

17

three layers of black clothing, and wiped off all my war paint. What was Gio's deal, anyway? What right did he have to make me feel like a total idiot? Oh, bloody boogers, I *had* been a total idiot, too, no getting around it. Forrest Gump had a higher IQ than me, that afternoon. Didn't Gio know who I was? I was Vick, the school witch. The tough girl! The bad chick! Damned straight!

I hopped into my Pooh nightshirt and crawled into bed. "Gio, you're going to be running in the opposite direction from now on!" I warned my stuffed Mrs. Tiggy-Winkle. I gave her a quick kiss before I turned out the light.

The next day was fine until after lunch, when I spotted Gio in the front hallway. "Vick? Where are you going?" asked Addy when I nearly collided with a plaster bust in my sudden flight away from His Supreme Blondness. Dermot would've had my hide for toppling over the statue of our school's namesake!

"The other way!" I choked out, fleeing.

Crapola, what in the world was *wrong* with me? For an entire year I'd worked so hard on being tough and unapproachable, and there I was, running for my life like a Russian aristocrat being chased by revolutionaries!

Normally whenever I step out into the hall between classes, all I need do is keep my eyes peeled for hazards in the route ahead. Athletes looking to make a little trouble. Hair Club girls anxious to score sarcasm points in front of their boyfriends. Those kind of hazards I was used to. Those following two days, though, were hell. I panicked every time I saw someone with spiky blond hair. Even the custodian's broom set me off, when I saw the straw bits poke out from the closet.

Vick, you're losing your edge, I told myself in the mirror that night. *Be tough! Be dangerous! Make him fear you!*

Yeah, myself said back to me. *I can do that. He'll be sorry he laughed at me!*

And don't mention virgins again.

Like that'll happen?

It happened before, you've gotta admit.

Oh, shut up.

You shut up!

No, you!

It was at that point I started to worry whether talking to myself was a sign I might really be crazy. But you know, a long incarceration in a mental institution, complete with daily shock treatments and ice-water enemas, sounded pretty relaxing and low-key compared to a single day at Fillmore High.

I finally saw Gio again the next day near the cafeteria, after a nerve-racking morning that would make the Spanish Inquisition look like sheer comic relief. "Hey!" he said, much too loudly. "Hey, don't go. I've been looking for you."

My arms prickled. My throat started to close. I hate being noticed—except, of course, when I'm deliberately looking for attention. Don't hate me because I'm capricious. "Oh, fudge!" I swore. I instantly regretted it.

He blinked. "Did you say 'fudge'?"

"Um." Eye of newt! Why did I turn into a screaming

19

ninny when Gio was around? "No," I told him. I toughened my hide. "Why would I say 'fudge'? Wanna know what I said?"

Even the F-word failed to convince him. He shook his head. For a second I thought he was laughing at me. "You don't seem the 'fudge' type; that's for sure. Come here; I've got something to show you."

I rolled my eyes. "The last boy who said that to me went home a new soprano. Not interested."

Gio had this weird expression on his face, as if he'd won the lottery and I was the first to know. It was like he and I shared a secret and he was totally geeked to be talking about it. Only I don't keep secrets with boys like him, and we were definitely not on speaking terms, no matter how goofy he made me feel. *Especially* because of how goofy he made me feel. He turned around so that his back was to the bunches of kids on their way past us to the cafeteria. "Look," he said, doing something with his hands in front of his chest.

"*Hasta la vista,* Roadkill." I started to walk.

"No, really, come here! I don't want everyone to see."

I was really getting cheesed with him by this point. What was he, some kind of obsessed witch groupie? Was he trying to give me the secret witch sign so I'd know he wasn't, like, a witchaphobe? "Listen." The annoyance in my voice was one hundred percent natural and all-organic. "You—"

Then over his shoulder I saw what he was doing. He'd made a circle with his thumbs and fingertips. Inside that circle, suspended in midair, floated a No. 2 pencil. It simply hung there. My jaw must have dropped wide, because on seeing my reaction he grabbed the pencil and faced me. "So now can we talk?"

Tongue firmly checked and arms crossed, I followed Gio as he led me outside to the end of Pop Alley. As I approached, kids scattered, leaving us pretty much alone. When Gio came to a stop at the last of the soda machines, he put his hands in his pockets, like he was trying to think of what to say. It felt good not to be the tongue-tied one, for once.

"I thought you'd like to use that trick." He shrugged. I raised a single eyebrow, something that took me absolutely forever to learn, but has been worth it ever since. Drives people absolutely batty. "Okay. Listen. I think you're good. *Really* good. You've got that whole"—he used his hands to gesture at my hands and face and outfit, and tugged at his ears. I think he meant my pentacle earrings—"going on, and you've got the reflexes and the misdirection down pat, and you've got this stage persona—it's incredible! You're great, like I said."

I had a sick feeling in the pit of my stomach, as if one of those chest-bursting aliens were growing there. "Great at witchcraft? Yeah, I am."

He went quiet, like he wasn't sure we were speaking the same language. "No. I meant . . . great at street magic."

Plainly stated, I wanted to cry, but I refused. It took every fiber of discipline in my body to force out one of the lamest sentences in the English language: "Say what?"

"Okay," he said, looking at me funny. "Let me tell you how I see it."

The scene felt like one of those stupid detective movies where a bunch of phony English types sit around the parlor while the little guy with the mustache explains how Lady Agatha was stabbed in a sealed room at the top of a locked tower during the masquerade ball that gave everyone an alibi. Except that it felt like the detective had already fingered me as Miss Scarlet with the knife in the lounge. I gestured with my hands. "Bring it. But I can tell you already that you're wrong."

Gio crossed his arms. We looked like some kind of wrestling smack-down commercial. "Okay. Here's what everyone else saw yesterday—some chick walks out here with a major 'tude. Suddenly out of nowhere she casts a spell. Words show up on her arms when she rubs a bunch of cigarette butts and ashes on them. Really smooth move, by the way. Disgusting, but smooth." I cocked my head. "But it's not what I saw, which was this: Same girl leaves the cafeteria, her sweatshirt half-off. One arm's invisible. I'd guess she has, like, a wax candle under there. Maybe it's on a string. But it's something clear, something sticky. Something she can write with, right?" He looked at me for some kind of confirmation, but I kept my neck rigid and refused to move. *Keep cool,* I commanded myself.

"So I'm thinking that while her left hand's invisible, she's using it to write something pretty generic on her right arm. Like, 'You're dead meat.' Could apply to anyone, right? Then she gets outside and it still looks like she's taking off her sweatshirt, because both arms are in there now. She takes a few seconds to write something on her left arm with the wax—the guy's name, now that she knows who's bothering her friend. Then the sweatshirt comes off and there she is, looking pretty good in a sleeveless top. Because the wax is clear, no one can see that she's marked up her arms already. They only see her ready for a fight. The trick's ready to go a long time before she rubs ashes over her arms and they spell out words. It looks pretty freaky. It looks like she's done the impossible. Here's the thing, though. It's not witchcraft. It's street magic." All during his speech I had wished he'd stop. Now that he'd fallen into silence, I had nothing to say to his challenge.

You know, it's funny. For an entire year I had dreaded this moment. Every time I knocked against someone for show or pulled off one of my "spells," part of me trembled inside, afraid someone might point a finger and yell, "Fake!" Gio was dead right on almost everything. He was the only person ever to see through my little scam and call me on it.

And it didn't feel like the end of the world.

Oh, yeah, it was bad. It felt like Gio had walloped me with a two-by-four, pulled my teeth out with a pair of rusty pliers, and made me rinse with Ty-D-Bol. I wanted to sink into the pavement right then and there and melt away like the Wicked Witch after Dorothy gave her a bucket shower. More than anything I wanted to run home and crawl into bed and *die*.

Despite all that, something in the back of my head told

me, *You're going to get through it.* That belief kept me on my feet, arms crossed, eyes unflinching. "It's this whole getup of yours that makes it work!" He had started talking again. "You're, like, really a pro!"

"Is there a point to any of this?" I found myself asking. Weird—I should have been afraid of him now, but he was being so *nice* to me. If Melinda Scott or any of those other high school harpies had seen through the fog of hair spray around their heads and figured out my secret, the elementary school kids in the neighboring town would know it by now. Gio . . . well, Gio was different, somehow, and I wanted to know why.

He moved a little closer. "Can you keep a secret?" All I had to do was raise an eyebrow to that one. Could I! "Okay. Go out with me tomorrow night?"

"Hey!" I said, instantly on guard. "Hey hey hey! Slow down, Romeo! Of all the sleazy—"

His reaction was classic scorn. "Nothing like that. I thought you might be interested as a professional. I guess I'm wrong." Gio reached into his shirt and detached the little device that had enabled him to do the floating pencil stunt. He bundled it up in his hand and held it out to me. "Here."

"What's this for?" I asked, accepting it like I would a live hand grenade.

"Use it sometime. You know. Let someone catch you floating something, then pretend they weren't supposed to see. Lend a little more mystique to your persona." He waggled his fingers in air quotes.

I turned over the little contraption of elastic and transparent wire in my hand. No one like Gio had ever before given me a gift. I looked back up after a moment. "What do you mean, interested professionally?"

"Come tomorrow and find out."

My hesitation was real as I stuttered out, "What time?"

"Seven." He grinned again. Cheddar on a Triscuit! I wished he wouldn't smile and catch me off guard! Moves like that made me half want to like him.

I curled my lip. "Listen up, buddy-boy. If your tongue trespasses on any of my private property, I'm ripping it out. It'll take care of that aggravating talky noise your mouth keeps making." He grinned at that and started to amble toward the cafeteria. "Hey, Roadkill," I called after him.

"Yeah?"

"A candle? You can do better than that. If I was the person doing that trick . . . *if* . . . I'd hide a wax pencil inside my sweatshirt. Available at quality craft stores everywhere, you know?"

It took him a minute to understand what I meant. Had I said too much? Would he despise me now? Gio smiled shyly and nodded at me, and, like magic, vanished through the swinging cafeteria doors.

CHAPTER THREE

Adriana Kornwolf is my very best friend in the entire world. That said, it absolutely kills me that she insists we sit with the good students near the front of geometry class when we could be having a perfectly good time kicking back at the rear. But noooooo. We had to be where Ms. McClenny could glare and clear her throat at me every time I whispered.

Her back to us, McClenny squeaked out some kind of proof on the blackboard. Addy used the opportunity to reach over and drop a folded-up wad of paper on my book. Inside, her neat handwriting asked the question: *SO??? Where did you and G. go?*

Addy knows simply everything about me. Everything, that is, except for the fact that I'm not really a witch, and I could never, ever, ever tell her that. Not now. She'd probably hate me for lying so long.

Here's my sorry story in a nutshell. Dad kept losing jobs—not his fault, but it happened. In four years I'd been to seven different schools in seven different states. Finally we ended up in this podunk city out in the middle of nowhere. I mean, once you reached the city limit here, all the buildings dropped away and you found yourself surrounded by nothing but farms and amber waves of grain. I'd been picked on so much that I'd already decided what I was going to do to keep people off my back at Fillmore. So when a geeky redheaded girl took pity on me the first day, put her lunch box next to me in the lunchroom, and asked my name, what came out was a lie: "I'm Vick. I'm a witch." My first words to Addy. Total black mark on my permanent record. How do you make that up to someone when they decide they like you anyway?

Sometimes I worried that I'd wronged Addy by letting her be my friend. She'd been a study grind before, and a geek, but even geeks were higher on the food chain than my little losers' club. I made amends by protecting her. No one messed with Addy. I saw to that.

"Ach-hem!" Diagonally behind me, Melinda Scott cleared her throat. She was trying to get the teacher to catch me passing notes, but McClenny was too busy extolling the virtues of pi, like pi was her dream boyfriend who not only did all the chores around the house, but made pizza every night for dinner and lowered the toilet seat after his business. Melinda narrowed her eyes and hissed at me, "Bart Nelson sprained his ankle yesterday because of you!"

"Oh, no!" Addy could be such a softy.

"And?" I shrugged, turned back around, and smiled

to myself. The best part about my so-called curses was that afterward, when people got bad grades and hurt themselves and flunked their driver's license tests and all the everyday bad things that would have happened to them anyway, they always blamed me. Bonus!

"*And* you're a sorry *freak,* that's wha—"

Ms. McClenny stood in front of Melinda's aisle with her hands on her hips. "Melinda Scott. You have something to share?" she snapped.

"No, ma'am." Melinda waited until McClenny turned back to the board before she stuck out her tongue at me. I've seen gorillas eating their own poo who managed to be less tacky.

Under Addy's question, I wrote a quick answer: *I went to his place and then we went somewhere else and hung out.*

My arrival at the Carson home was a little bit like Cinderella, pre-makeover, storming the prince's castle. That is, if ol' Cindy had been dropped off by her dad in his ten-year-old econobox with the busted muffler, and if she'd been wearing a big black T-shirt with a tarantula printed on it to match her spider earrings. Oh, yeah, and if the prince's mom saw said raggedy car and T-shirt and decided the girl standing outside looked like she'd come to beat up her son.

"Won't you come in?" said Mrs. Carson, trying to recoup from the *oh-my-God* face. She was one of those hair-spray types who wore nice conservative shoes around the house. Shoes! Around her own house! "Gio!

Your . . . friend is here!" she called up the stairs in a cultured tone, like moms on television.

The Carson place had everything. Big wide-screen television in the living room. Antiques. Real paintings on the wall in real frames painted gold. The decorations were museum reproductions like you'd see in fancy catalogs. I made a resolution right then and there that Gio would never see inside my house. Not when the fanciest thing Dad and I had was the tiny little television decorated with Disney World mugs on top. Definitely out-middle-classed, I felt hot and embarrassed and kind of wished I'd made more of an effort. For a minute Mrs. Carson and I smiled nervously at each other. I knew the second I left the room, she'd haul out the Lysol and spray everything I'd touched.

Gio didn't seem to think I looked out of place, though. "Hey!" he said from a stairwell lined with engravings of ancient Victorians on horses. "Come on up!"

When I reached his room, it became obvious Gio was the castle's prince, complete with a king-size bed to his name. He had a television bigger than the one downstairs, connected to some stereo system that looked like a *Star Trek* spaceship computer. All sorts of clothes spilled out of his closet; shoes peeked from under his bed. An electric guitar reclined on a stand. Stacks of video game discs nearly obscured the computer on his desk. A giant old-fashioned poster of Houdini hung over his bed. A basket of fresh laundry sat on his chair, decorated with a little note: *Hope I got the grass stains out of your jeans! XO, Mom.*

Gio was definitely a boy handed life on a platter. For a long, sickening moment, I wished I could trade places with him.

"Hold on a sec." He started looking for something while I stood there gawping at his stuff. What else was I supposed to do? Ask for decorating tips? The only really good thing I could say about my bedroom was that at least the leak over the doorway only really got bad after it had been raining for an hour or more. "Now, where is it?" He started rummaging through the already messy pile in his closet until he found something toward the very back. It was a hat—actually, a white towel wrapped around a cap and stuck with a great big jewel in the middle so it looked like a turban. He put it over his spiky hair and grinned at me. "Ta-da!"

Okay, what kind of kinky mess was this? "Um, listen, Roadkill. If you're expecting me to dress up like *I Dream of Jeannie*, I'm gonna make you a eunuch. For real."

Addy brought me back to geometry with a kick. McClenny was saying, "Who would like to come to the board and . . ." She cast a speculative look in my direction. *Aw, crud!*

The door opened. *Saved!*

It was Vice Principal Dermot. *Curses!*

But he had someone with him, and she surely didn't look like a hall pass to the principal's office with my initials on it. *Saved!*

I wasn't saying any of this aloud, was I? Whew.

"Good morning, class." I'm sure the Doormat knew it was a worse morning for us than for him. He was just

30

rubbing it in because he'd never have to take geometry again. "What a *fine,* fine day! No doubt you are all *feasting* at the banquet of knowledge." Twenty-five pairs of eyes that would rather be at home, in bed, watching the Spring Break Crisco Twister finals on MTV, regarded him bleakly. "It is my pleasure to introduce to you a fellow aspirant to edification. An addition to the sophomore class, recently transferred from . . ." He seemed to falter. The girl leaned over and whispered something. "Yes, of course. Los Angeles, California. Well. Isn't that nice. Miss Brie Layton."

Los Angeles? That was where Dad and I originally started out. Who else would move to this godforsaken place from L.A.? This was the sort of small city where even the biggest dreamer thought small and longed to escape to a bustling metropolis like Sioux City or Omaha. It wasn't a place where anyone *wanted* to live.

Addy rolled her eyes as the new girl walked in. She liked chilly blond girls about as much as I do, which is about as much as I'd like an entire series of rabies shots. You know, though, I had been a new kid so many times myself. Kids criticized everything from my face to my hair to my clothes to the way I walked. Somehow I felt a little sorry for New Girl as she endured everyone's stares. Brie wore the clothes of someone who'd dressed for success but found herself thrown into a pigpen. Her skirt was a little below the knees, her perfectly trimmed hair was below her shoulders, and judging by the curl of her lip, we were obviously way, way below her.

"I hope you will make her feel welcome." Holy cannoli,

was the Doormat still talking? At his cue, Brie Layton assumed the kind of smile you might see on a January snowman walking into an industrial deep freeze. Frosty. Very frosty.

Typical that Melinda Scott fell for it, though. Brie's big-city glamour must have been like chum on the water for her. I heard a little *tap-tap-tap-tap* sound behind me and saw her patting the empty seat on her far side. I hoped Brie enjoyed having the rest of her high school life organized by the Hair Club set. She'd sure get a lot of yearbook appearances out of it.

She must have seen me studying her as she passed. Brie pulled up the left half of her lip and sneered back in my direction. "Don't mind the sideshow exhibit," I heard Melinda stage-whisper, while Ms. McClenny dug in the closet for a textbook. "She's a nobody."

"I guess every school has its *charity cases*." Oh, Brie was going to fit in fine, I could tell.

I looked her dead in the eyes. "Nice. Very nice, coming from someone whose parents named her after a particularly slimy *cheese*." Melinda goggled at me. Brie turned red. I mean, molten-lava-itching-for-a-virgin-sacrifice red. For a second I felt awful. I must really have hit home with that stupid remark.

"What's *her* ready-for-*Oprah* trauma?" Brie asked her new friend as I twisted back around.

Melinda rolled her eyes. I was sure Brie would get an earful later. Addy waited until class had returned to normal before dropping another note on my desk: *Went out WHERE? What did you DO???*

Just to this club. It was okay.

Yeah, it was kind of a club. A club for, like, senior citizens. Picture me with a wrinkled old woman in a wheelchair on my right. She had to be at least five hundred years old and was so feeble that the plastic oxygen mask on her face kept threatening to drag her head to her chest. On my left was an old man in his bathrobe whose eyes were closed and who kept snoring and resting his head on my shoulder. We were in the Shady Pines Nursing Home's finest auditorium, a tiny room that also doubled as the cafeteria and the afternoon nap room. About fifteen of us watched Gio onstage. Me and the crinklies, whooping it up and having a good old time, only without any whooping or good time that might accidentally pull out someone's life-support system.

Okay, now picture this: Gio wearing that ridiculous, horrible turban and a cape made out of some fringed tablecloth, on the stage in front of a poster showing the five steps of CPR, doing magic tricks. He did pick-a-card-any-card illusions, coin tricks, and pulled scarves out of people's ears. He made jelly beans appear and passed them out to the members of the audience who weren't snoring. He linked and unlinked solid metal rings, and then finished his act by sawing a Barbie doll in half and restoring her right before our very eyes.

Here's the thing: He was awful. He was *bad*. There's something every magician knows called palming—you use the ball of your thumb to tuck something in your hand while making it look like you're not—and Gio really had no talent for it. When he was pulling quarters out of

33

seniors' ears, I could see the coin a long time before it appeared. When he performed card stunts, his hands were so slow and clumsy that it seemed he was only one step ahead of remembering how the trick worked.

I can't tell you how much I've practiced over the years. I'd spent hour after hour every day in front of my mirror at home mastering moves. That trick where I grab someone's homework and rip it up? It took three weeks of work at home just to get down the bit where I make the switch between the real homework and the fake notebook pages. Two or three hours a day, working on that one move, watching myself in the mirror and trying not only to make it look natural, but to make it look like I hadn't done anything at all.

Gio's family might be wealthier than mine, I realized. He might have all kinds of equipment from the magic catalogs. But he didn't know jack about how to make those tricks his own.

Mr. Iverson is always going on and on in English class about something called irony. You know, like in that stupid short story about the chick who shaves her head and sells her hair to buy her boyfriend a new watchband or something, while the boyfriend hocks his only watch so he can buy his girlfriend a stupid comb. It's pretty obvious these people are, like, in serious need of a Christmas present counselor. Who even *buys* hair?

Anyway. The irony here was that as bad as Gio was, these old people loved him. If he'd been tapioca pudding, they would've eaten him up with a spoon and licked the floor to get every single last globby bit. They didn't care that during the Barbie trick, the cabinet door opened halfway and you could see Barbie cooling her tootsies against the table while Skipper's cut-off legs poked out the bottom of the box. The California Raisins didn't seem to mind that Gio spent two entire tricks with his elbow clenched against his side, some old man's card tucked under his armpit, so he could pull it out and surprise him with it later. They were clapping and smiling and grinning from ear to ear and cheering him on in a way I sure never got at school.

He was awful and got cheers. I was perfect and got nothing but avoidance. That's irony, and no one had to sell any hair for it.

"You young people are absolutely wonderful," the great-great-great-grandma next to me said, once I had pulled down her oxygen mask for her. Even I was kind of enjoying myself at that point. You know what was best? Gio kept grinning at me the entire time. It was weird at first. I'm not used to anyone *looking* at me. Then it got kind of funny, like we were sharing a joke that all these tricks were obvious and bad.

Afterward, though, when all the old people thanked him and the cafeteria staff gave us little half-pint cups of vanilla ice cream that we ate with flat wooden spoons, we found ourselves alone. I was sitting on top of his magic trunk and he was in a chair opposite. "How long have you been doing this?" I wanted to know.

"Magic? Since I was a kid. I put on shows for my folks and my older brother until my mom got tired of her euchre decks disappearing all the time. She knew someone at a Boy Scout troop, so I did a show for them. Then it was a few little kids' birthdays, and an Elks Lodge thing, and I've been coming out here once a month for the last year."

"They really love you," I said. Watching them beam at his every move really warmed me. I wanted that kind of approval. If there was anything I wished for, it was a little recognition for my hard work.

"Thanks." He got serious. "So . . . do any of your friends know . . . ?"

"What, that I'm not really a witch?" Ow. I'd said it aloud for the first time ever. It felt bizarre. I sucked on my little ice cream paddle to stall my reply. All the fun I'd had in the previous hour disappeared the moment he prodded at my sore point. Finally I said, "No. They might let it slip. I can't have that."

"You don't do it for attention, though. I've watched you. It's like—"

"My act makes people leave me alone." I watched his eyes as he studied my hair and my clothes and my shoes. For the first time he really seemed to see me as I was. When he stood up from the chair and turned away from me, I felt a sick, cold feeling wash over me.

He'd realized what a freak I really was. He was going to say something polite and distant, then get rid of me as quickly as possible. It was over. Why had I said anything? Crud!

Gio turned back around and sat next to me on the trunk. "Nobody knows I do this kind of thing either," he said, really slowly. Relief washed over me. I could tell he was revealing something very private. I'm the master of concealment, after all. "None of the kids, I mean. It's nerdy. It's nerdier than being a *Star Trek* geek. Even if I were any good at it, people would think it was . . . I don't know. So lame."

Apparently he did know how clumsy he was, then. At least I wouldn't have to pretend. And he hadn't said a word about me being a freak! "Do you practice?" I asked. "I mean, in front of a mirror?" When he looked totally blank, I had my answer. "Look. You've got to really *work* to make those palms as smooth as silk, or no one's going to buy them. Like this." I produced a wallet from thin air.

He stared at it for a minute, then finally got a clue and snatched it back. "That's mine!" We exchanged a very real grin. What was left of my coldness began to ebb away. I liked him. I really liked Gio. But how did I know if he really liked me back?

His tone was shy when he said, "Listen. I have some ideas for you. You don't have to use them. I do a lot of reading. I've collected lots of books. I thought with your showmanship and my help . . ."

I got where he was going. "And I'd help you out in return? Show you a few moves?" He nodded. I thought about it for a minute. It was a real risk for me. I'd always worked solo. What if he screwed me up, or ratted me out? I could make him practice enough to eliminate screwups, but trust—that was something I wasn't used to. I wanted to be around him, though. I might hate to admit it, but my decision was already made. "Yeah. That would be pretty cool."

If anyone ever doubted I was a good magician, they would have changed their minds after the trick I pulled off then: I managed to keep my face totally blank and cool, as if nothing big had happened, though inside I felt like I'd won the lottery. I made a silent prayer, though— something I never do. *Please let him not be pulling some sort of scam*, I asked the big guy in the sky. I didn't think I could stand to trust someone and have them betray me.

I unfolded the new note that appeared in the crease of my geometry text. *You are so not telling me something!*

Oh, man. If only Addy knew.

CHAPTER FOUR

My first ever magic show I saw was from backstage. When my mom was still alive, she once had a bookkeeping job at a Los Angeles bowling alley where bands would play on a little stage at one end. Sometimes, if Dad was working nights, she'd bring me along to the alley to sit on one of the benches and watch people bowl while I waited for her. I was, like, maybe eight years old.

One night a magician took the stage. No big name or anything—just some local guy with an incredibly cheesy mustache and a pretty little assistant. Because I knew the place, I managed to get backstage to take a better look. For most of the show he made scarves disappear. I yawned my way to the finale and only really paid attention when he said he planned to levitate his assistant. After a lot of hooey-gooey about harnessing the mystical powers of the cosmic forces, he had the assistant lie down on a table with wheels. He threw a sheet into the air and let it billow down.

Just as the sheet settled on top of her—or what I thought was her—I saw the assistant roll out from a trap-door in the table and under the back curtain. She dusted herself off, walked back to where I sat, plopped down beside me, and asked me if I knew I was the cutest little thing in the whole wide world. Meanwhile, onstage, Mystical Mustachio kicked the table into the wings. The body under the sheet floated! But from where I sat, I could see black threads holding it up. While the assistant chewed a stick of Juicy Fruit, she tugged on the threads to make what looked like her body, float higher and higher.

Finally the magician reached up and whipped off the sheet. The audience gasped to find the girl gone. Well, no kidding! She'd been right next to me, popping her gum in my ear the entire time! Within a few seconds, though, she reeled in from the rafters what had been making the sheet all curvy with girl parts—a folding frame made out of black wire.

That was when I realized there were really two entirely different shows on that stage. The drunk bowlers in the audience saw a woman floating upward by magic, then disappearing into thin air. The show I saw was where all the hard work was done, and that had taken place before the sheet had settled over the wire form. After that, the magician talked a big game to make his audience think they had seen something miraculous.

I blabbed so much about that magic show that my mom went out the next day and bought me a book of magic tricks. I started practicing immediately. That book turned out to be the last gift my mom ever gave me; she died six months later. I stuck with the magic after that. I don't know why. I guess that no matter how much things hurt, knowing I could palm a coin or pick someone's card made me feel like I had a little control over my world.

At eight, I thought magic was the coolest thing in the entire world. At sixteen I still did. Gio *got* that. He totally got off on how fun it really was to trick people's eyes. It made me feel good. Good, but worried. He might have figured out my secret, but I still didn't know how much I could trust him with it.

"I have an idea," he said to me later that week, up in his room. "Have you thought about that Houdini movie I showed you?"

I looked at the poster over his bed. Ol' Harry hung upside down from some kind of hook three stories over the ground. It was obvious that although he looked like a smokehouse Virginia ham, he was about ready to bust loose and send the crowd below into rapturous applause. Houdini, the great escape artist! "What about it?" I asked, getting a not-rosy image of hanging upside down from the school flagpole while the cool kids pelted me with rolls from the cafeteria and hair scrunchies.

"It's kind of a scandalous trick. If you get it right, though, everyone will be talking about you. Pull off a couple of the things I have in mind, and you'll be a living legend."

He looked at me expectantly. A living legend? Me? I glowed inside. It might feel good to have people marvel at me for a change. "Tell me."

41

While he explained how the trick would work, I began to worry that Gio was some total sicko setting me up so that everyone could mock me. You know, like that movie where Carrie went all psycho prom queen on the guy with the bad perm and ended up with a pig's blood corsage and a bucket for a crown? Gio couldn't be that kind of person, could he? No one would go that far for a joke. Right?

I surely hoped not.

"I don't know," I told him. I don't usually like admitting to anyone when I'm scared. Gio's plan was pretty freakin' weird, and all I could think of was how the school bullies would be making me lick crusties from the rest-room toilets for the next two years if it failed.

"Hey." When he hopped up on the bed next to me, I shied away. "I know it sounds risky. But come on, think of the payoff when it works out! You will be the official hands-down shout-out baddest witch Fillmore High has *ever* seen." Once again he grinned at me.

I'd never had anyone admire my skills so openly before. It was almost intoxicating to have them recognized. "Okay," I said, keeping my face expressionless. "But you've got to practice."

"Sure!"

"I mean, *really* practice. Two hours a day on the rope part *alone.*"

"We can start tomorrow. Your place?"

"No!" There was no way I could ever let him see my house. "Here."

He shrugged. "I've got no problem with that." I wished

42

I had X-Ray Spex for the soul. Could I trust him? There aren't any sure answers in life, I guess. If I was going to buddy up with him, I was going to have to take a chance and see what happened.

I bit my lip and agreed, and thus was born:

THE INCREDIBLE FEAT OF THE AMAZING
VANISHING HIGH SCHOOL SOPHOMORE
PERFORMED IN THE PEERLESS STYLE OF H. HOUDINI
(IF HE HAD GONE TO THIS GODFORSAKEN HIGH SCHOOL)

Okay. I said there were two parts to a trick. There's what the audience thinks it sees, and what actually happens behind the scenes. So here's what my audience saw:

Dude, you know that ugly freaky girl? The witch? Okay, get this. So she's walking down the hallway after lunch, down between the shop and the band room. Guess who's behind her? The girl with the scabby face and then the fat one. God! Why do they let people like that in the school? Are the sideshows full or something?

"Hey. Watch this." One of us sticks out his foot as she walks by. Dude, the witch goes flying! Her books land in front of the band room door across the hall.

"Nice one, Gio!" we tell him with a high five. It really was cool to watch that freak bite the tiles.

"Have a nice *trip?*" asks Gio. We had a good laugh at that. Gio's cool—fits in with everyone, never makes a fuss, doesn't rock the boat. Everyone likes Gio.

It's kind of funny, the way Fatty and Scabby try to help her up and pretend like nothing happened. Shame she had to get up. More fun to walk all over her. "Real mature, anal wart," the witch says. "I haven't heard that one since, what, second grade?"

Real mouth on her, that one. She goes over to pick up her books, and a few of us guys follow her. Her little sideshow buddies are helping her, looking all nervous, like they're gonna get beat up. And maybe they are, you know? "You can't talk to us like that," one of us tells her.

She gives us a snotty look. "Trust me, if I were talking to you guys, I'd have to use little-bitty words of one syllable."

"Witch."

"She ain't really a witch."

"She cursed Tyler Woodwell and he broke his leg and was out for the autumn games," said one of the cheerleaders.

"Yeah, and after she faced off with Jason Munro, he got caught with that fake ID."

"Listen," said the witch. "The Roadkill and I are having an *A-B* conversation here, so if the rest of you would *C* yourselves out . . ."

There were about seven of us, four guys, three girls. It's real funny how the freak backed away when us cool kids moved forward, real slow. Laugh-out-loud funny. When she realized she couldn't get around us, she ran into the band room.

"Not so funny now, is it, huh?" said one of the girls

as we followed her. "Look—she's scared!"

"Whatsa matter, Broom-Hilda?"

The girls cackled with laughter. "Come on, Glinda, show us what you've got!"

"She ain't got nothing."

The freak spoke up. "I've got more than any of you could ever handle."

"Ooooh, feisty!"

Someone from the back spoke up. Gio again. "If she's so tough, she can curse us from inside the instrument closet." Ha! Good old Gio! The witch looked all scared and stuff while Gio closed the door to the band room and then from the wall ripped down the Fillmore Mountain Goats marching flag. "Hold her," he said. Two of the girls jumped to obey him—who wanted to pass up a chance to get back at the witch?

It was funny how quick it all happened. Gio unhooked one of the gold ropes from the flag and wrapped it around her wrists, getting it real tight so she couldn't move. Then, while she was still swearing at him, a couple of the other guys took the Mountain Goats marching-band banner and threw it over her head. It hung down almost to her knees, it was so big. She kept jerking back and forth, like she honestly thought she had a chance of getting out.

"Trapped!"

"And that'll take care of *you!*" Gio took the other big rope still hanging from the banner and wrapped it around the witch's middle. Dude—she wasn't going anywhere! Then the girls shoved her into the instrument closet. Bam!

Someone banged the door shut, and then Gio flipped the shackle and slammed down the padlock. A couple of us high-fived each other. Too funny!

"Loooooooooser," one of us yelled at the closet.

You couldn't even hear a thing from inside. That's how thick that door was. She was gonna be in there until dinnertime. Maybe overnight. I mean, hell, who cared if she was missing? And it's not like she could climb on her broomstick and fly out, right?

We were all hopped up from the rush of it. "Did you see how she looked when we got her? She was all like, *Oh, don't hurt me!* and we were like, *Get out of my face, freak!* and she was like, *Whatever!* and we were like, *We're gonna get you!* and she was all, *Hocus-pocus!* and we were like, *Yo! Take that!*"

One of us cracked in a real high, squeaky voice, "Are you a good witch, or a bad witch?"

That's when . . . here's what they saw next:

That's when I stepped through the door of the band room and leaned against the frame, all cool and collected. "Best witch you'll ever know." I smirked.

Their faces simultaneously drained so white that it was as if I'd activated a Blood Sucker 2000 under the band room floor. When one of the big bruisers finally opened his mouth, he swore in a high soprano, as if I'd actually grabbed him by the ghoulies and squeezed. "But you're in *there!*" he squealed. "We got you!"

I examined a fingernail before replying, trying not to

look at Gio and totally give the game away. He was doing a good job of acting himself, at the back of the pack. "Yeah, you got me, all right. Got me in a mood to cast a few curses." Before they could answer, I stepped forward and crossed my arms. Gio had been right. I savored that moment more than any other I'd had in my long, sad school history. "Next time, guys, save the games for Milton Bradley. And don't screw with me again."

Finally, here's what they didn't see:

There's an old-fashioned movie of Harry Houdini from, like, the Dark Ages, where three big goons use a rope to tie him to a chair. For a whole minute and a half they wrap the rope around his legs and neck and shoulders and head while he wiggles around like someone's put itching powder down his back. Then the brutes leave. While the camera's still running, ol' Harry stands up, jerks a couple of times, and the ropes kind of slither to the floor.

If Houdini could pull off that trick with a twenty-foot rope, Gio pointed out to me, a few feet of silk cord was going to be cake. When you wiggle and tense up and bend your wrists so that there's extra space between your forearms, it creates slack. When you relax, the ropes relax with you. Leave enough slack in enough places and boom, you're Houdini, those ropes dropping all around you when you stand.

Still, although it was easy enough to lure that mixed gang of thugs in the direction I wanted, I wanted Gio to tie my wrists. All his secret practice in his bedroom tying me up—that sounds a lot kinkier than it actually was—

47

really paid off. I admit I had a quick moment of doubt when Gio really got into his part and the rope seemed a lot tighter than what we'd practiced. If ever he was going to betray me, that was the time, all right.

The second after they had that heavy marching banner over my head, though, I had my wrists free. They couldn't tell. Though I was still pretending to fight and struggle, I mentally breathed a sigh of relief. Gio hadn't been setting me up, after all.

That length of rope they tied around the banner? Same Houdini principle. After they pushed me into the instrument closet, all I had to do was push off the banner with my freed hands. The ropes dropped in a clump around my ankles.

From there it was a quick climb up the big wooden shelves where the band students stored their instruments; then I pushed open the trapdoor in the ceiling that no one ever seemed to notice. To make certain none of my attackers saw my escape route if they opened up the door again, from the ceiling grating I covered the space below the hatch with a big square snare-drum case. It was thick enough that it wedged perfectly between the top shelf and the trapdoor. Then from inside the ceiling crawl-space, I dropped the hatch.

There's a whole world up above our heads in that school that no one knows about—vents, pipes, tubes, and a bunch of walkways that maintenance people use for repairs. A quick run, and then I dropped through a twin trapdoor into the janitor's closet across the hall. All that was left was to make a grand reappearance.

The entire stunt had been planned well in advance—from scoping out the maps of the walkways in the dropped ceiling space two weeks before (they're pasted up in practically every janitor's closet—but who ever goes in there?), to planting the extra-big drum case on the top shelf, to making sure the latch was open on the trapdoor across the hall so that I wouldn't be caught up in the near-darkness. Once the ropes were off my wrists, my real work was done.

"What the devil is happening in my school?" Lordy, Lordy. There are some things you can't plan for, and the Doormat was one of them. He stuck his bald little head through the door. Atomic clocks could've kept time by the throbbing vein on his forehead. "None of you are *in* the band." The vice principal then noticed me standing apart from the others. His face contorted, as if he'd discovered a pimple on his butt that had passed the blobby purple stage and had graduated to oozing pus on his Fruit of the Looms. "Marotti. I should have known you'd be involved."

"Tell them to let her out!" I heard Dorie's frantic voice from the hallway. When she pushed her way in past Dermot, she was actually crying. For a second I felt irritation—I've told those kids time and time again, no matter what they say or do, crying tells bullies they've won! At the same time, I was grateful she cared enough to fetch help. She blinked to clear her eyes, saw me, and got that same look as the others. "Oh!" She looked torn between wanting to throw all one hundred and seventy pounds of herself on me, and screaming at my impossible escape.

49

Desiree crept in behind her, a thin line of blood on her lip where she'd gnawed at it. "How did you *get out?*"

The Doormat looked as if the entire lot of us had River-danced on his very last nerve. "Get out of what?" he snapped. "Someone had best explain to me what is going on, or I'll be seeing you all in deten—"

From the back of the crowd, Gio stepped forward. "I'm sorry, sir," he said. "Marotti and I had a few words. It shouldn't have happened."

"More than *words!*" sputtered Dorie.

The Doormat held up a hand, cutting off the outraged *shoooooo!* sound that Des had started to make. He gave Gio a level look. "I admire a man who can admit to his mistakes," he finally said. "If more people were honest like you, Carson"—and here he gave me one of those *like you!* looks so blunt you could've used it to hammer railroad spikes—"this school would be the kind of place I'd be pleased to send my own kids. If I had any."

"i'm sorry, sir. It won't happen again." Gio turned to me and stuck out his hand. The vice principal nodded with approval. I curled my lip slightly before I shook.

Everyone else saw two opponents pretending to make up. I'm sure the Lord of the Flies crew thought Gio was faking the apology as much as the Doormat probably thought my part in it was bogus. The real show, though, was only for me and Gio. Our hands touched at the same moment our eyes met. I seemed to feel an almost electric shock pass between us. We were both trying like mad not to grin our heads off at each other. I saw happiness on his face, and pride, and real excitement, and it kind of made me feel shy to know he probably saw the same things on mine. I certainly felt them.

We unclasped our hands. While he swaggered back to his little gang, I rolled my eyes at Dorie and Des to let them know what I thought about boys like him. "I don't want to see your face for the rest of the week, Marotti," snarled the Doormat like a bulldog when I eased by.

Down, boy! Have a Scooby snack, already! "I don't think that will be a problem, Vice Principal Dermot, sir," I said sweetly. Considering it was nearly one on a Friday afternoon, I could probably live up to my end of that particular bargain.

A crowd attracted by Dorie's crying had gathered outside the door. Good. Word would spread more quickly with people around. "Well, well, well," I heard off to one side. "Wasn't that a Kodak moment!"

Gah! Melinda the Hun! And her new flunky, Brie, carrying one of the yearbook-staff cameras! I tried to walk by, but they were determined to get a rise out of me. "I'm not sure I'd waste the film," said the new girl.

I was still flying from the highlight of my career, so it didn't take much to make me swing around. "What a nice pair you make. Cheese and Crackers. Couldn't ask for a better combo! Buh-bye now!" I got a savage satisfaction at seeing Brie darken with anger again.

But it was nothing compared to the balm I felt at seeing Gio, his blond head bobbing and ducking among the crowd of bullies we had duped, smiling at me as I left.

CHAPTER FIVE

"Boy, did you see how he ran from me?" I asked Addy, looking back over my shoulder. Bart Nelson's retreating form hobbled in the direction of the exit. "Edit that. Limped away."

"Yeah." Yeah? A "yeah" from the queen of complete sentences? Something was different about her. She sounded upset.

I raced to catch up with Addy as she pushed her way through the crowded cafeteria. "Hey! Wait up!" I called. She instantly stopped in her tracks near the end of the food line, frozen. She didn't turn or anything. Just stood there until I caught up. This wasn't the Addy I knew. "What's wrong? Was someone picking on you? Was it Bart?" They had been standing close when I scared him off.

"I know you're itching to curse someone, but no one was picking on me." Was it my imagination, or was Addy bringing the snark to our conversation? Maybe I couldn't

52

hear very well over the screaming kids everywhere, but that wasn't like her.

"Come on, then!" I jerked my head in the direction of our usual rendezvous.

I had loved walking around school those two days after my disappearing act. Heads would bend down to whisper in ears. Rumor would follow rumor. Pretty soon I'd find everyone staring at me like I was some kind of Marvel superhero who'd forgotten to remove her flashy costume before going back to her wimpy, normal, everyday life. What a rush! Sometimes I saw envy in their stares. Sometimes I'd see fear. Either way, they had all stopped looking at me like I was doggie doo someone had trampled in.

No, I was the hot-diggety-dog, the head honcho, the big bad, and everyone knew it, baby. I could've made a sudden move for the comb in my pocket and terrified kids around me would've hit the dirt. I was a celebrity, and I was loving it. Okay, so no one asked me for an autograph, because it would've been scrawled in cigarette ashes on my arms, but hey. A witch can't have everything.

My lunch was only a sandwich and a pop, so I hauled them from my backpack and gave a quick greeting to my fellow losers. Addy sat on the bench at the end of the table and set down a sack lunch, from which she pulled out an apple, a roast beef sandwich, and a bag of crackers. It seemed like there was an awful lot of room around her. She sat there rubbing a tissue over the apple, her

53

back to the cafeteria, almost seeming to pretend she didn't know any of us.

"Hey," I said, finally realizing why we had so much room. "Where's Hello Kitty?" I'd never seen her bring her lunch in a paper bag before. Weird!

"Home."

I expected more explanation, but it wasn't coming. "Did someone steal your lunch box?" Already in my head I was plotting my revenge. I jutted out my jaw and looked around the lunchroom, already picking out the suspects. One of those Hair Club wenches, maybe, or maybe one of those band-room bullies trying to show me up by getting back at my friends.

"Stop it!" Addy's voice was surprisingly loud over the babble. "Sit down. Stop it." I was surprised not only at how crabby she sounded, but also by the fact that when I'd looked around, I'd risen halfway out of my seat. I plopped back down and stared at her. I mean, really stared at her. She was red and flustered—she gets flushed too easily—but there was a way she gnashed her teeth into her sandwich that meant she was really, really mad at me. The other kids at our little Island of Misfit Toys developed sudden interests in their lunches. Ray let out a long sigh. Dorie filled her mouth with cafeteria pizza.

I raised my eyebrows at Desiree, who'd begun to use her teeth to tug at what was left of a fingernail. She got the message and put her hands in her lap. "What is your *deal?*" I asked Addy. While I glared at her, I realized what

I'd overlooked. No wonder she appeared different! "Your hair. You cut it."

"Friday," she snapped. She must have had it cut the evening of the band room incident, and I had been so wrapped up in myself yesterday that I hadn't noticed at all! I was the worst friend in the world! The change wasn't minor, either. Addy's hair used to be a dark red helmet of frizz that she sometimes tamed into pigtails. Now it hung down straight and smooth, the leading edges pulled behind her ears. It was very hip. Very classy and fashionable. In my self-absorption, I'd totally overlooked it.

Weird—but when I realized my mistake, I raged at her for a moment. What in the name of *Cosmo* gave her the idea to go glamming herself up? She'd gone further than the hair. She was wearing eyeliner and lipstick, and her light freckles were invisible under a layer of concealer. But why? "Hey, it looks great!" I forced myself to say. "You look really . . . really . . . really great." Why was she changing?

With the glare she gave me, you would've thought I said that it looked like she'd been pulled from the back end of a cow and left to dry. "Nice of you to *notice*. I forgot my milk." She tossed down her sandwich and stalked off in the direction of the half-pint cooler.

Desiree made a *mmmm-mmm!* sound at me as I stared after Addy.

"Okay, so I didn't notice it yesterday," I said. "Sue me. I saw it today!"

Ray gave me one of his stares of contempt. "It's not

only the hair, fool," he said. "It's not even just yesterday and today." I shook my head. I didn't know what he meant. "You haven't been around much. When you're here, you're not really *here.*"

Ow. That really stung. What the heck?

"You used to hang out with us after school. Addy says she hasn't seen you for two weeks," said Dorie.

"Everything I've been doing has been for you guys," I said, my chest heavy as I spoke. I hate when people make me feel defensive. I hate it! "If I haven't been around much, it's because I'm working on my skills so these trash-holes will leave us all alone!" There. That wasn't a lie. I meant my sleight-of-hand skills, of course, but they would think I meant my witchcraft.

Ray shrugged. "Addy's your friend. You should spend time with her." I opened my mouth to do the point/counterpoint thing, but Ray shrugged. "I'm just saying, is all." He went back to stroking the silky fuzz on his upper lip.

I sat back against the wall and felt increasingly huffy. When Mr. Iverson isn't going on and on in English class about irony, he's talking about this thing called *subtext* that's supposed to be, like, everywhere. He says that everyone has this really deep subconscious that makes us do stuff without knowing why. Like Hamlet. Is he grumpy and to be or not be all over the place because Uncle Claudius married his mom, or is it because he really wants to be man of the house himself? Or that Oedipus guy, the old Greek. Did his subconscious know all along that he'd killed his dad and married his mom? Come to think of it, there were a lot of characters in English class that were kind of freaky about their moms. Does that mean there's some kind of subtext to Mr. Iverson we should know about?

I *so* didn't want to go there.

Anyway. I couldn't have been more cheesed if my last name were Kraft and I wore shoes carved out of Velveeta. I don't know much about the subconscious, but I knew exactly what was bugging me about Addy and her haircut. It killed me to admit it. I would have rather blamed my sudden black mood on a hundred excuses rather than on the one thing I knew, way deep down inside, bugged me most.

I was afraid of losing Addy. I worried that all it would take to wing her way out of the losers' club was some new hair and a little bit of makeup. It sounds stupid, but the kids in school are so superficial that way. *Addy is different,* I kept telling myself. She'd never cared what I looked like in the past.

What if all that time I'd spent with Gio had made Addy think she wasn't my friend anymore? Oh, holy heck. That was exactly why she'd been so cold to me lately. Could she be on the lookout for new friends? Was that what this hair business was all about?

When I came back from my thoughts, the babble of the lunchroom and the stench of sloppy joes felt like a sudden shock. I almost kind of expected to see an emergency rescue squad standing over me with electric paddles, and all my friends still yelling, "Don't go into the light!" I wondered if the panic in my eyes was, like, totally obvious, because Ray and Des and Dorie all immediately turned their heads from me, embarrassed.

It hurt like a thousand cats sharpening their claws on my shins, but I pulled my face into a smile when Addy came back to the table with her little square carton of milk. "Hey," I suggested, "I'm going to the mall after school. Wanna come?"

It was a lie; I was supposed to go to Gio's, but he'd just have to deal with it. Our practice could wait a day. I had all of seven dollars to my name, but I could always say I was looking for an outfit that none of the stores sold, and not spend anything. Addy sat back down and made a big deal about opening her milk and putting a straw in it before answering. "Why would I want to go to the mall?" I could tell she was interested, but that she wasn't giving in quite yet.

Okay, I could do the carrot dangling thing. "Because of cheese-on-a-stick," I told her promptly. "You love cheese-on-a-stick. Mmmmmm. Cheese! On a stick!"

She looked primly at her sandwich. "I have to finish my history project."

"Hamburger-on-a-stick too," I said in the same voice that mermaids used to lure ships onto the rocks so they could suck the sailors' blood. Or was that vampires? "And a blue lemonade. I'm buying. Oh, come on. It'll be a nice, normal time." I turned on the wheedling. "We can try on makeup and see what kind of new outfits would go with your hair!" When she shrugged, I could tell I almost had her. "And ice cream after." Maybe Ray would lend me five.

"Well . . . okay," she finally conceded. Over a bite of roast beef, she looked up at me and smiled really shyly.

I saw the others relax. When my mom was alive, she and Dad used to have big old arguments about money sometimes. Not all the time. Enough for me to remember, though. Dorie and Des and Ray looked relieved—like I used to after the argument was over and Mom and Dad were at that kissing-and-making-up stage. For a moment I felt kind of weird. Did they think of me and Addy as kind of substitute parents? I wasn't sure I wanted that sort of responsibility.

I have to admit that I looked forward to that afternoon like I usually looked forward to Friday-morning math exams. What if Addy was standoffish and cold? Was I going to have to spend the entire time trying to get things back to normal?

There was a little of that at first. After we got off the bus and started walking around Arcadia Mall, which is about the only thing in this town that passes for real shopping, there were a few moments when I thought I wanted to shake her. I kept bringing up topic after topic and only getting halfhearted answers from her. What was I going to have to do to get back in good with her, throw myself on the floor and beg?

I very nearly did. But then a miracle happened right there in the middle of Urban Shoemeisters. I started talking about how totally freaky it would be if Mr. Iverson and Ms. McClenny were, like, going at it in the teacher's lounge together during lunch, when lo and behold, she giggled. Then it kind of developed into a goofy little reenactment of them macking down on each other like kids behind the bandstand at prom. By the time it turned into a little *Passions*-like melodrama with Mr. Iverson trying to figure out how to unhook a bra, and me acting both parts, Addy had tears in her eyes and was begging me to stop. I grinned at her. She grinned right back and wiped her face.

Things felt right after that. I decided to do some schmoozing while the schmoozing was good, and gave her a lot of compliments about her hair. In return, I got a lot more information than I ever wanted to know about what the hairdresser had said while she was getting it lopped and straightened, and a long, long list of what conditioners she was using now. It was cool, though. She was talking to me like I was her friend again, and we were joking and teasing each other like nothing had happened.

It was halfway through the second cheese-on-a-stick that she finally brought up the one topic we'd avoided. "So, okay," she said. "I don't get this thing with Gio. One week he's, like, Mr. Perfect with the hair and the clothes and taking you out to a club and everything, and the next, he's a total butt monkey—" She put a hand over her mouth and widened her eyes, surprised those words had come out of her mouth. "No, but all of a sudden he's, like, this total butt monkey who's beating you up and locking you in the band closet!"

"Oh." Not for a minute had I forgotten that Addy was the only person in the entire school aware of any connection between me and Gio. Even during our secret after-school practice runs between the band room and the janitor's closet, Gio and I had been careful never to be seen together. I'd hoped Addy wouldn't ask this particular question. "I only saw him twice before I had to . . . you know."

"Dump him? Is that why you haven't hung out with me? Because you were down?"

She looked hopeful. It would be so easy to lie to her and win her forgiveness. "Yes," I said before I really thought it through. I regretted it instantly, but it was too late. "I needed some time. You know how boys are," I said, looking down at my blue lemonade with what I hoped was the sad face of an older but wiser teenager. I was an awful person, but the lie was easier than the truth. "And how they are when you won't . . . you know . . . do things they . . . want you to."

I thought Addy would get angry on my behalf. I thought she might comfort me and tell me it wasn't my fault. What I didn't expect was for her to turn the color of a grape sucker and stare at her lap. Man, I must have really mortified her! While she continued to keep quiet, I managed to work up a little irritation. What, maybe she didn't think Gio could go for a girl like me? Why wouldn't he?

Why *hadn't* he, actually?

Okay, so there was the little thing where I'd once threatened to make him a eunuch if he laid a finger on me. But you know how boys' hormones are always short-circuiting their brains so they forget everything but the one track their minds are on. If Gio had to remember anything I said, why *that?* Did I want him to . . . you know . . . try something? That was the tricky part. *No,* my brain kept telling me. *Keep it strictly professional. Remember what love's all about. Stupid pop songs. Swapping unsanitary spit. Grossing out your friends.*

Inside me, though, part of me kept saying, *Yeah. But . . .* Maybe it was my subconscious.

"Oh!" said Addy, completely jumping topics. "When we're done, can we go to Glitz 'n' Giggles so I can get some Hello Kitty pencils?"

Hallelujah! Addy still liked Hello Kitty! There was a higher power!

It was while we were in Glitz 'n' Giggles, happily picking out pencils and stickers for Addy while wearing stupid decorated eyeglasses, that I saw them. "Crapola!" I shouted, making a beeline for the window. I peered over a stack of stuffed alligators, fairly confident that no one would recognize me. Not wearing a pair of enormous purple spectacles covered with rhinestones and a feather at each temple, they wouldn't.

"What?" asked Addy, surprised at my outburst.

"Cheese and Crackers. The Hair Club on wheels." I pointed to where two well-dressed backs sashayed their way down the main corridor of the Arcadia Mall, their well-groomed hair swaying with every high-heeled step. "Wenches."

"You know, calling them stuff is as bad as when they call us names." Addy peered out the window beside me.

"Don't go there. Not the same at all." I watched Brie and Melinda smile at each other with big ol' Colgate teeth. "They're so fake. I bet they spend an hour every morning on their hair and makeup."

Addy straightened up. "I don't think it's nice." A touch of the lunchtime coldness had crept back into her voice, but I was too busy trying to figure out how to take advantage of this situation.

"Holy cats!" I had an idea. I watched the two give each other a look, say something, and pause in front of Music Metropolis before they went in. "Catch up with me," I shouted as I ran for the door.

"Hey hey hey hey!" I heard the store owner screech, right when I got there. Addy yelled out something too, but I was a girl on a mission.

"Oh, crud!" I yelled. I'd forgotten about the Elton John specs. I tossed them onto the counter with a sincere "Sorry!" and ran out the door. Truthfully, I needed a couple of seconds to myself. Stalking their trail like a bloodhound, I made my way over to the instant passport-photo booth halfway between the Glitz 'n' Giggles and Music Metropolis, watchful that the terrible twosome didn't suddenly pop out and see me. I ducked into the booth and pulled the curtain shut.

It took a moment for my eyes to adjust to the darkness. Okay, I was alone. I pulled out the wax pencil from inside my T-shirt where it hung on an elastic band and contemplated the insides of my arms. Or how about my forehead? I hadn't done that one in a while. No, I didn't want to have to ride the bus home with DIE, BRIE! on my forehead for everyone to see. Should I pretend to curse both Brie *and* Melinda? Or just Brie? Because frankly, Brie's snotty L.A. 'tude was getting on my very last nerve.

I'd finally decided on a choice threat for Brie when the curtain was yanked open with a sudden flood of light. The elastic band snapped my wax pencil inside my shirt when I released it. I yelped as it smarted my skin. "Thanks for *ditching* me," Addy snapped.

"Ssssssh!" I told her. "I'm spying on them."

"I finally managed to convince the Glitz 'n' Giggles owner that you're mental, and not a klepto." Despite all those four-to-a-strip photos you see of happy couples making faces at the cameras, those booths are not made for two people. Addy scrunched down with her shopping bags beside me on the little bench as best she could. I had a sudden sympathy for sardines in a tin. "Can't we just do the stores?"

"You know we can't shop with them around. They'd be all, 'Ooh, look at the freaks. Trying to better yourself, freaks? Trying to be one of us?' Let me scare them off and we'll have the place to ourselves again."

"A nice, normal time, you said. You promised."

If I could've put my hands on my hips and stared at her, I would have. In that cramped, sweat-sock smelly, dark place, I had to settle for a sharper tone than I usually used. "Listen. I'm doing this for you, you know." Silence. Good. I'd finally gotten through to her. "Stay here while I check them out. I'll be right back."

Addy's voice was very small, though she sat right next to me. "I came out because we were supposed to have a good time. I could be finishing my history project, you know."

"Don't be ridiculous," I told her. Didn't she know after all this time that I was going to take care of things? "I'll only be a minute. I'm going to check them out and then you can watch some witchy goodness. It'll be a *great* time."

It was nice to breathe fresh air again, I have to admit. What I really wanted to do was scope out the area so that I could maneuver Brie into a spot where the trick seemed effortless and unplanned. A big planter sat right across from the Music Metropolis, I noticed—its soil would adhere perfectly to the wax on my arms. All I'd have to do was get Cheese and Crackers over in that direction. If I could collect Addy, hide around the corner from the store entrance where we could keep an eye on it, and make it seem like we *happened* to bump into them . . . Oh, yeah. Perfect. I trekked back to Addy.

"Come on," I said, ripping open the photo booth curtain. "They're still in there. We can . . . Addy?" The booth was empty. "Addy?" I looked around. Where had she gone? I'd told her to stay put. People pushed by me as I looked around wildly. I felt lost. Where was she? I couldn't see her at the Day-Ree Twist or the luggage store. Had she misheard me or something?

I peered down the side hallway, blinking against the late-afternoon sunshine pouring through the plate glass. A city bus pulled to a stop in the circle. When it blocked out the blinding rays, I saw a little figure with red hair standing there, all alone: Addy.

"I think we're going to have to start shopping somewhere else, don't you?" I heard a voice say in a drawl.

"Well, ye-eah!" Brie looked at me and then looked away.

"I didn't know they were letting a certain *low* element in these days."

"I guess someone missed the memo saying freaks should stay in the circus."

Oh, boy. Oh, boy. I had to make a quick decision. Either I stayed to curse the Doublemint twins and let Addy escape, madder at me than she had been since lunch, or I chased after Addy. She was getting on the bus right that moment.

There was only one right thing to do. "Hey, Mozzarella," I said to Brie. "Tell your buddy that when she came out of the rest room, she tucked her skirt into her panties." Melinda let out a shriek and whirled for a peek at her behind. "Look up 'gullible' in the dictionary sometime, would you?" I sneered before I hightailed it out of the mall.

Any triumph I might've savored from that encounter, though, vanished in the vapor of diesel fumes still hovering in the empty circle. I was too late. Addy had gone home without me. For a minute or two I stood there, hoping against hope I'd been mistaken. I wanted Addy to walk around the corner, bags in her hand and hair back in pigtails, to tell me it was all a joke.

She didn't. It wasn't. It was me and an empty bench, waiting for the next bus home. For nearly an hour I sat alone and watched people walk into the mall to have a nice, normal time.

CHAPTER SIX

I don't know how many other people have stared down a goat before. Not me. In my little contest of wills between girl and beast, the goat was definitely winning. Gio's laughter didn't help things. "Oh, my hat!" he hooted. "When you said you didn't have any experience with animals, I thought you were exaggerating."

"I've never even owned a *goldfish*," I complained, digging my heels in and tugging. The goat glared at me and resisted until the second I relaxed my pull. That was when he lunged at me. His teeth—if that's what you called those massive incisors of death trying to rip the flesh from my bones—snapped and gnashed. My eyes watered from the blast of goat breath. That alone was enough to make anyone give up. I hollered and fell backward into the dust. "Stop laughing! It's got weird devil eyes! And I've smelled full baby diapers that I'd rather use for perfume!"

"It's a goat, not an air freshener." I stood back as Gio

marched over, grabbed the goat's collar, and tugged. It took the goat only a moment to decide that Gio was the kind of guy worth following and more or less obediently amble beside him around the pen.

I leaned back against the fence. "I think it can tell I'm a big-city girl. How do you know so much about goats, anyway?"

"It's my grandfather's farm, doof," he told me. "I used to have to spend whole summers here. Goats aren't the most obedient creatures in the world, but— Ow! Stop that!" Gio jerked away his hand when the goat tried to go all Cujo on him, too.

"What if Rambo the mountain goat is worse than this one?" I asked.

"Rambo the mountain goat is a kitten. All he does is eat and sleep."

"A kitten, huh?"

Gio raised his eyebrows, pursed his lips, and curled his hands up under his chin like little paws. "Mew."

I laughed long and hard at that one. Gio made jokes easily. I liked that a lot. During school hours I noticed that people were always laughing at his friendly, teasing comments. Some people are naturally relaxed and funny, you know? It was his personality. Here we were in the middle of a goat pen on a farm twenty miles outside of town, just the two of us, and he was as much at ease as in his room or walking down the hallway at school.

I envied him that ease. I wished I could be comfortable once in a while. The closest I came was when I was around him. Gio made me feel almost as if I could relax.

He gave me permission to let my guard down a little. I could joke with Addy—until recently, anyway—and with Ray and the others, but I could never really *relax* when they were around. I was always on the lookout for them. Gio didn't need protecting.

"What if Rambo the killer mountain goat attacks me? I can't handle this ugly punk!" Rambo's the school mascot. He's not really a mountain goat, since when he's not being used in school projects or appearing at the occasional homecoming, he spends his vacations being coddled on a highly unmountainy farm outside town, like this one. I don't suppose he's ever killed anyone either, but how in Helsinki was I supposed to know?

"Vick." Gio gave me the look I'd come to know meant he wasn't taking any nonsense. "Trust me. I was in 4-H. All of us know that Rambo is about the dullest goat ever born. He's positively ungoaty."

Gio and I worked really well together, though. It took time, but that evening he finally got me to the point where I could steer his granddad's goat without yelping and flinching like a girlie-girl. Did he want more than working together? Did I want more? Romantic stuff, I meant. Or was that one of those topics I wasn't supposed to address? Man, life was so much *easier* when it was just me watching out for people.

It was funny how Gio and I complemented each other as a team. Every hour of practice we shared improved his technique. After working with me, he could even keep a card hidden without clutching it in his armpit. He'd lost the annoying habit of following his misdirections with his own eyes. Sleight of hand is all about making people think they've seen something they haven't; it's about palming coins and hiding gadgets and pretending they're invisible. If you draw attention to them with your own eyes, well, you might as well hang up your top hat and put the bunny away, because your audience will never believe anything you do ever again. If you create the right misdirections, though, the audience is yours to command.

Take the trick we'd planned, for example:

THE MYSTERY OF THE AMAZING DISAPPEARING RAMBO
THE KILLER
(WHO ISN'T REALLY A KILLER)
MOUNTAIN GOAT!
(WHO'S NEVER BEEN ON A MOUNTAIN BUT IS DEFINITELY
A GOAT, HOWEVER UNGOATY)

Heck, I bet David Copperfield would give his left nipple to see this one. Here's how it worked.

First there's the setup. Real stage magicians have it easy. They get huge Las Vegas stages with smoke machines and eerie music. All those guys, though, get tons of money thrown their way so they can set up the premise of the trick and make it work.

I have to make do with what I have—lockers, out-of-date textbooks, my geometry compass and protractor, and smelly sack lunches. And my premise? Inside I might have felt like a confused idiot who didn't know how many beans make five, but on the outside I was all about being a tough-talking mistress of dark forces with fingers itching to do some devil's business.

So. I walked down the hallway real slow one Friday morning, the day of the last football game of the school year. I'd dyed my hair a shade blacker the evening before, and spent the evening perfecting an expression meant to imply I could freeze lava with a single glance and munch on diamonds like they were Tic Tacs.

Then I saw them. The football boys. I'm not saying they're all bad; there are a lot of guys on the team who play hard, study, and stay the heck out of my way. There's a smaller crew, though, who act like they've found their Holy Grail: to get into the Fillmore football squad and wear the team jacket.

For most of us, high school is some kind of dentist's waiting room in hell, one building north of the twenty-four-hour drive-through slaughterhouse, across the street from the Bad Hair Eternity Salon, a little bit east of the Michael Jackson Brimstone Memorial Fountain. For these guys, though, high school is the real shiznitz. It's their peak. Everything else will be downhill after it. They'll be hanging together in twenty years, picking their noses and wondering what happened to the good old days when before afternoon practice they could grab some helpless kid, drag him to the boys' room, stick his head in the john, and give him a swirly.

I can't stand those guys. They think they're some kind of elite little club too good for the rest of the world. They make trouble for those of us who only want to get through the day. I steeled myself for the encounter, though, and kind of sauntered up to where five of them lounged in front of their lockers. Then I crossed my arms, leaned against the row of metal doors, and waited.

Arnie Peterson was cupping his palms like he was about to pitch two giant basketballs. "I almost had to call in backup. Dude, I'm tellin' you, she was *enormous.*"

A couple of the jocks laughed like the spineless bobbleheads they are. The others were already nervously looking my way.

"Oh, *real* nice," I said. "Maybe if I'm lucky and wish upon a star and learn to sew and cook and mop up trails of puke, my prince will come, and he'll be one of you romantics."

Arnie dropped his hands. "Whatsa matter, Marotti," he wisecracked, "decide to hang out with the big boys when you found out Ray wasn't *man* enough for you?"

"Ow!" Tyler Woodwell twisted his face in a fake grimace and shook his hand as though Arnie's witticism had stung. He should've known better after getting cursed into breaking his leg last semester. "Houston, we have a crash-landing!"

While a couple of guys made jeering noises, I pouted prettily like one of the Hair Club girls. "Come on, meatloaf-for-brains. Everyone knows Ray's got more between her legs than any of you."

Tyler laughed for a second until he realized that this time he was the one on the receiving end of the wicked stick. "Hey!" he protested. Idiot.

Arnie approached me by a couple of steps. The other guys backed off. Five football players, all taller than me by six inches minimum and two or three times my weight, against little ol' me. Yeah, I'd say we were pretty evenly matched. "I'm not starting something with you," he told me. "None of us are."

"Yeah. Just back off, Broom-Hilda!"

I kept the rest of my muscles still while I turned only my head to look at the fool who'd dared to speak—it was a move I got from one of the *Terminator* movies. I didn't know Thad Johnson all that well, but he was one of those loudmouthed freshmen who hadn't learned when to keep his mouth shut, obviously. "Oh, you've asked for it now," I said in a low, mean voice.

Quick as a flash I slammed back Thad's locker door so that the loud bang made everyone jump. Tyler shrieked like a kiddie. Inside the door Thad kept a hanging pad of sticky notes. A lot of us have them hanging there—the school gives them to us in our orientation packets every fall, and they're handy for quick scribbles and that kind of thing. While everyone watched, I ripped off the top sheet. It had some girl's phone number on it. Typical.

"Dude!" Thad protested.

"Shut up," Arnie told him.

While I folded up the little paper, my lips mumbled a magical spell. If anyone could actually have heard, it would have sounded a lot like "Gio Gio Bo Bio Banana Fana Fo Fio Fee Fi Mo Mio . . . Gio!" but I kept the volume low. Without warning I flung out my fingers and made the paper disappear. A couple of the guys gasped at the sight of my seemingly empty hands.

Then with my left index finger I pulled up the tip of my

nose and reached into a nostril with my right finger and thumb. Within a second I'd seized a folded-up square of paper and pried it out. "Gross!" breathed Thad.

I flipped the paper open and held it taut with both hands. There was the girl's phone number, just as it had been before. When I flipped my hands so they could see the other side of the paper, scary red letters spelled out, YOUR LUCK ENDS TONIGHT!

The guys looked like one of those games of skill at the state fair. I could've pitched quarters into their open mouths and won myself a blue teddy bear. "You are *so* cursed now, boys." I casually sashayed away, a certain bounce in my step.

"Dude," I heard Tyler say when I was at a safe distance. "She didn't have her hands anywhere *near* her nose until she went digging in there!"

Well, of course I didn't have my hands near my nose. I didn't need to. Five minutes before, in the privacy of a girls'-room stall, I'd shoved the prepared curse up my nostril. Like I said, all the kids have those sticky notes in their lockers. When I positioned my hands so that my audience couldn't see the edges of the paper, how was anyone going to be able to tell I was holding up the preplanted curse back to back with the phone number I'd palmed? Two pieces of paper—but their eyes saw only one.

Man, this audience was easy.

At a school in Cleveland last year, I got an A in biology for a report I did on the human eye. Either it was pretty good, or the teacher was stunned I turned something in. You see, every second of every day our corneas and irises take in millions of bits of information about light and texture and color and motion. The brain's really good at processing all that information . . . but it's not perfect.

Magic's not about what the eyes see. It's about what the brain *thinks* the eyes see. In the split second when the brain's processing all that information, it's possible to fool it with suggestions. Tonight's stunt, for example, needed only three suggestions. The first was my threat to the football team to lay the big supernatural smackdown on their sorry padded behinds. That was all taken care of, and quite neatly, too. Gio and I had to finish the stunt with two more simple suggestions: one to the eyes, and another to the ears.

A worry. A sight. A sound. Their primitive pea brains would take care of the rest.

That was how later that night I found myself in the school gymnasium, huddled behind a bank of tall black wooden boxes holding the reserve bleachers, while the football team had its pictures taken by the yearbook staff. Rambo slept in his cage on the other side of the bleacher boxes, awaiting his big Kodak moment. Boy, could that goat snore. Not loudly enough to drown out conversation, though. Personally, rather than endure all the buttkissing and fake compliments I had to hear from my hiding place, I would've rather spent my evening armed with only a tiny dollhouse spoon and my teeth, assigned to clean toejam from an entire crew of burly construction workers done for the day. Blindfolded. In the nude. On network TV.

It was disgusting. From the yearbook girls it was all,

75

"Oh, Kiefer, you look so handsome in your uniform!" this, and, "Are those pads or are they your *muscles?*" that. You could practically hear all the crispy gelled hair crackle with hormones when the testosterone strutted into the room.

I heard a voice nearby. Since the tone was so snotty that you could've caught it in a Kleenex and sent it to the Centers for Disease Control for analysis, I automatically knew it belonged to Melinda Scott. "Do I have on too much gloss?" she was asking. "I've got on too much gloss, don't I? I saw it in the store and I was, like, *so* all about this color that I couldn't stop putting it on, but now I've got too much!"

"You look fine." Oh, great. Brie Layton, too. They must have come into the gym through the open door closest to me.

"Ohmigod, lookit Tyler!" DeMadison Cook always imitated Melinda's singsongy voice as closely as possible. "Is he, like, looking at me? Oh, God, what if he looks at me? Is he looking at me?"

"He's not looking at you," said Brie, sounding irritated.

"Oh, hush, DeMadison. Brie, we have *got* to *get* you a *boyfriend,*" Melinda told her. They sounded near. Too near. Why in the world were they standing so close to me and Rambo the killer mountain goat? They were supposed to be with the rest of the yearbook staff, down at the other end of the gym where the lights had been set up.

"I'm pretty sure I could find one myself. If I wanted one."

"Goats are *smelly!*" DeMadison announced. Well, yeah. She might have had the brain activity of a particularly stupid carrot, but I was with her on that one. Rambo's stink would've made anyone wish for a bushel of incense and a goat-sized spray bottle of Chanel No. 5.

"Where's your camera? I want a photo of me with Alan and Arnie. I'm thinking, like, inside-front-cover material. Brie, you are *so* lucky you hang with us instead of with some of the *losers* around this place. I swear, you are, like, the luckiest girl in the world!"

There was a little clatter at my feet—the slightest sound, really, but it made me jump in a panic. It didn't take much stretching my neck to see that one of them had dropped a lipstick to the floor. Holy cannoli!

I froze. I already had my dark shirt's hood pulled up over my head to help keep me concealed, but I still didn't want to make any sudden movements. What if they found me crouching back there? The whole trick would be blown! Crispy critters, I had to think of something fast in case they caught me.

"I'll get it." Brie sounded as uninterested as before. From the corner of my eye I watched the narrow strip of floor visible to me. My heart pounded like a full rehearsal of the Mountain Goats' drum section practicing during a thunderstorm. I saw a pair of bending knees, a swoop of hair, and then a neatly manicured hand retrieving the escaped lipstick. Did Brie see me? Did she notice? I held my breath until her hand disappeared. "Here you go."

"You're a doll," I heard Melinda say. "I hate when that happens."

"No problem."

A boy's voice cut into the conversation. *"Hola, chicas!"* I recognized the voice as one of the senior team members: Barrett Symms.

"Get your hand *off* me!" squealed DeMadison, annoyed.

"Sorry, dude, but it was either you or the goat, and you're a lot prettier." DeMadison's giggles could've curdled cream, I swear. "They're gonna start the photos soon. You gonna come watch? I need a pretty face out there to make me smile. Yeah, I mean you, babe. Hey, Rambo. Hey, Rambo!" I could tell Barrett was peering through the netting hung over the field-hockey goal doubling as a cage for the team mascot. "You gonna make us win tonight, Rambo?"

Now, I really can't say that Rambo the killer mountain goat understood English, but his noisy reply was perfect. I've never really heard many animals let one rip, but to my untrained ears it sure sounded like goat farts were among the most lethal stink bombs ever invented.

And the smell. Holy cats! The military should harness the deadly power of goat-butt gas as a slightly less destructive alternative to nuclear bombs. Seriously. You could use one of those puppies to incapacitate a city's population without actually killing anyone. On the other side of the bleacher boxes, I heard a buffet assortment of noises—gagging, coughing, retching, cursing, and gasping for air.

"Sheeeeeeeeeee!" growled Melinda. "Why'd you have to upset it?"

"I didn't upset it! I just said hey!"

"Ew, ew, let's *go!*"

It didn't take much in the brains department to realize that all the scattering noises and shrieking were Hair Club girls running to the other end of the gym. Someone remained behind, though. I heard the zip of a bag's fastener, followed by a deep sigh. "Yeah," muttered Brie to herself before she trailed behind. "I'm the luckiest girl in the world, all right."

When old people talk on and on about their blood pressure, I never pay attention. I mean, geez, if I need something to put me to sleep I'll turn on C-SPAN, okay? But after the kids left the vicinity of Rambo's netted cage and my hiding place nearby, I felt a little less like a balloon that had been pumped so full of air it was starting to lose its color. My heart stopped thumping like something supernatural out of an Edgar Allan Poe story, and went back to its usual unnoticeable beat.

In my dark little hidey-hole, it felt like forever before I heard clicks and joking and mutterings at the other end of the room. The photo session had begun. At last it was time to perform my part of the Amazing Disappearing Rambo the Killer Mountain Goat stunt.

One of the convenient things about all those flashbulbs popping every five seconds is that for a few seconds, the bright lights blind the people being photographed. When I peeked my head out of the bleacher boxes, the guys on the football team were the only people facing my way. With their eyeballs bleached by the light and from one regulation basketball court away, not a one of them noticed my black-gloved hand reaching out to the wall. No one saw me flipping the two leftmost switches to turn out the lights at my end of the room.

I pulled back my hand, sat on the floor, and waited once again.

There's a special kind of black fabric used in stage shows that changes appearance depending on how it's lit. When there's light on both sides, it's transparent. Oh, sure, you can still tell there's fabric there. It's not invisible or anything. But it looks like a normal sheer fabric. When there's only light shining on its front, though, it seems opaque. You can't see anything on the other side. It looks like a curtain.

Hold that black fabric against a black background— say, for example, some boxes used to hold spare bleachers—and without that backlighting, you can't see a thing behind that fabric. The eye sees lots and lots of black, and the brain confuses the fabric with the background and thinks it sees an empty expanse of darkness. Want to make the space shuttle disappear on national television? Cover it with what looks like a black net on a black tarmac and while the magician's distracting the audience, cut out the lights behind it. The net and tarmac blend together. Poof! The shuttle's gone!

Only it's not. Not really.

I held my breath and listened hard to the conversations at the other end of the room. This was the part of the trick that depended on fooling their eyes. Part of me wanted to poop my Pampers. What if Rambo chose this moment to neigh or whinny or whatever the heck it is that goats do? The longer it took them to notice, the greater the chance something would go wrong. Gio and I had thought we were smarter than a crate of diplomas when we'd dragged in the field-hockey goal, positioned it in front of the black boxes, and covered it with the special netting. We'd thought we were cleverer than a sack of cats the first time I'd turned out the lights and he gulped and reported he couldn't see me behind the net at all. All it would take was one mistake, one more goat fart, one person actually *crossing* the room, and the entire thing would—

"Okay, guys. Why don't one of you get the mascot and we'll take some shots with him," I heard the school photographer call out.

I froze. There's always a moment when you wonder if the audience is going to buy the trick, or whether you'll have to think fast on your feet to find a way out of a tight corner. This was the moment that would cement my reputation as a school legend, like Gio promised.

There was absolute silence for a second that made me feel sick to my stomach. Then suddenly it was as if someone had held up a cue card for a studio television audience reading: HUBBUB.

"He was just there," I heard one of them say over the babble.

"Yeah, he was just there!"

I heard Arnie Peterson's voice over the rest of them. "It's that witch!"

Yeah, I thought to myself. *It's the witch, all right.*

Then from the hallway I heard it: the noise. The sound

of a goat bleating. The acoustics of lockers and hard tiles made the noise echo and fade. A goat was wandering the empty hall, crying out. Of all the people on that basketball court, only I knew that the sound came from Gio, using a little novelty device we'd found in a toy store. It was really only a paperweight that made a goat sound every time it was turned over.

Like I said, there were three elements to this trick: a worry that I'd do something witchy to sabotage tonight's game; the sight of a seemingly empty cage; and finally, the sound of a goat in the hall. Their brains went to work and came up with the simplest possible story. That was all it took to trick an entire football team and a few people from the yearbook into thinking that Rambo the killer mountain goat had fled his cage and was running down the hall.

And if that hadn't been enough, Gio surely did the trick when he ran yelling at the top of his lungs through the far door of the gym, "Hurry! He got out behind the football field!"

The team yelled and scrambled. The girls screamed and followed. The people with cameras knew a good photo op when they saw it. They grabbed some equipment. It took less than forty seconds for the gym to empty.

I peeked out from behind the boxes to make sure the coast was clear. I have to admit my palms were sweaty. So many things could have gone wrong, but they hadn't. The tough part was over, and I was on my way to being a high school legend. Now it was time to make Rambo *really* disappear—and that would be easy as pie.

CHAPTER SEVEN

When I find out who first thought pie was easy, I'll have a bone to pick with them. I mean, all I've ever heard about piecrusts is how temperamental they are. You look at one with crossed eyes and it falls or explodes or whatever the heck it is that piecrusts do, right? And the filling! Who wants to pick all those apples or cherries or blueberries, get the bugs out, and stew them into a sticky mess? What sane person spends time on a pretty latticed crust top or on decorations that look like leaves? It's a mess, all of it.

But if Martha Stewart, revving up her ovens to make nine thousand solo homemade gooseberry pies for the annual Fight Third World Hunger Worldwide Bake Sale, had appeared before me right at that moment and said, "Honey, want to swap places? It's a good thing," I would have *so* taken her up on it.

"Come *on*," I snarled to Rambo. What was it with me and goats? Did I give off some odor that made them obstinate? Was my chewing gum made of goatsbane and

I didn't know it? The goat and I had made it most of the way down the hall from the gym. The band room and rendezvous point were only two dozen feet away. And then suddenly Rambo gave me the weird devil eyes and started huffing air through his nostrils like one of the Hair Club girls having a kitten fit. He absolutely refused to move.

Sure, it was kind of dark and we weren't easily visible. This part of the school, however, was supposed to be off-limits on game nights. All it would take was one flip of a switch, or someone with good eyesight to spy us from the gym, and there we would be: me and Rambo, in our face-off. "You are so coming with me," I growled at him. Once more I tugged at his lead, and once more Rambo stiffened his legs so that his hooves somehow dug into the tile.

Up until now, the entire Amazing Disappearing Mountain Goat spectacle had seemed like a lot of fun. It was our next big stunt—the way Gio convinced me I'd become top dog around this place. All we had to do was get Rambo back to his pen on the opposite side of the school grounds.

With the goat in our hands and the football team scouring the stadium out back, this was supposed to be the *easy* part. All I could do was panic. I felt as if someone had thrown cold water over me to wake me up from a nightmare, and my sleepshirt and sheets were still soaked and clammy. How in the world had I gotten here?

By saying yes to Gio's schemes, part of me answered. *You wanted to be a legend.*

I'd kept my profile low around this school before I met Gio. Sure, I threw around major 'tude and occasionally cursed someone. That used to be enough for me. Why did I tell Gio I'd do this kind of nonsense? I'd never been so stupid before.

Because you like him, you big buttchop.

But I wasn't one of those girls who lost track of all sense because of a boy, was I?

I groaned. Oh, man. I was! I was a classic goober who fell for a guy and let it get in the way of everything else, including common sense. Here's what bothered me: bad as I pretended to be, inside I was really a *nice* girl. I never wanted to be part of the perpetual detention crowd—in fact, I started using sleight-of-hand tricks so I could *avoid* confrontations that would end up getting me in trouble. I could imagine the look on my dad's face when I came home expelled for screwing around with the school mascot. We couldn't afford private school. What if we had to move again after he'd finally found a steady job?

Holy cats, what was I *doing* here?

Right at that moment I heard something in the distance. It could have been Gio doubling back to the rendezvous. Or it could have been one of the football players on the hunt. The thought of the latter made me grab Rambo's collar once more and start pulling. "Stop that," I told him when he huffed out more disgusted air at me. When I tried to haul him toward the closet, his rump seemed superglued to the floor. "You are the most uncooperative goat ever born!"

Far away, where the end of my corridor met the hall

running by the gym, I heard loud words. For a second I thought someone was shouting at me, but when I looked up in a panic, no one was there. I recognized the voice, though. Hooooo, boy. Did I ever recognize the nasal vocal stylings of Vice Principal Dermot! How could you *not* recognize what sounds like a cross between a high-speed dentist's drill and a cranky baby?

My heart beat faster than a Hi-NRG deejay at the turntables when I swooped down on Rambo the killer mountain goat and grabbed his neck in a headlock. "Listen," I growled into his ear. "You and I are going to take a little walk down the hall, see? If you refuse, I'm going to the kitchens to find some genuine Ginsu knives so I can carve you up into goatfurters and goatchops and goat jerky and I am *not kidding*."

I don't know whether it was my elbow's grip on his little barnyard windpipe or the threat to open up my own band room slaughterhouse, but Rambo looked sideways into my eyes and decided I wasn't kidding. He lifted his rear end from the floor and let me haul him the few remaining feet down the hallway to the closet, where I shut the door behind us so that we were hidden and alone.

Alone, in the dark.

Alone, in the silence.

Alone, with an animal that smelled as if it had taken a bath in Satan's dirty toilet.

There's a funny thing about being in a dark, enclosed space all by yourself. You start to think about how you have to pee. Then, while you're trying to think about anything else but your bladder, your mind wonders what it's like to be in a coffin. Dead. Because your dad killed you after you got expelled for stealing a goat. You listen for any noise other than the sound of your own raspy breathing and a goat stomach grumbling or goat teeth munching on the janitor's mop. I thought I heard footsteps outside several times, but the door was so heavy that it was hard to tell if I was imagining things.

Weirder still, you start to talk to yourself. *You could walk away right now,* some part of my brain told me. *You could get out of this closet and let the goat go and walk out of this building and no one would ever know you'd been involved in this entire mess.*

No one except Gio. Gio would know I'd deserted him.

You're always looking out for your friends, stupid. Why aren't you looking out for yourself?

Gio and I were a team. I'd agreed to this stunt. Following through was the right thing to do, wasn't it?

'Shyeah, if you want to end up in a juvenile detention center where they make you wear a blue smock and to use the phone you have to give cigarettes to some hulk named Big Marie.

"Shut it!" I snapped at myself.

"Okay, okay!" A rush of air from outside cooled me and relieved the goat odor. When Gio eased into the closet, I was surprised to find my eyes were closed. How long had I been sitting there, talking to myself? It was impossible to tell in the dark. "Let me get in here first."

I can't begin to describe how much my mood improved with Gio around. I couldn't really see him in the blackness. Even with the door cracked, it was barely any less dark than it had been before. I could smell him, though. He didn't smell like a little boy, all dirty and unwashed. He didn't smell like someone's dad with too much cheap cologne. He just smelled like Gio . . . like soap and acne pads and the faintest hint of nacho cheese corn chips. When I stood up to make room for him in the closet, the Gio smell blotted out all that goat funk. "You should close the door," I told him. My heart started thudding again, but I wasn't in the least scared anymore. Some other force made it beat so relentlessly.

"It's stuffy in here. We're going to leave in a minute," he said. "It'll be okay. Are you all right? How's Rambo?"

From the way that Rambo was jostling for space in the tiny cupboard, a blind man could have told that his health hadn't suffered any. "Gio, we've got to talk," I told him. "I've been thinking about these tricks we're doing, and I think—"

"Ssssh." I saw the silhouette of a finger raised to his mouth to shush me, and then of his head as he leaned back to listen at the crack in the door. He waited a moment before talking. "Thought I heard something. It's okay. They're all on the other side of the school, anyway. But hey . . . you should be happy! It couldn't have gone any better!"

"It could've gone all wrong!" I said back, keeping my voice low. Right then Rambo bleated out a complaint and decided it would be lots of fun to stick his snout in my butt. It was so much fun that I nearly screamed, but at the last minute I remembered myself and pinched shut my mouth.

Lurching forward against Gio, though, was entirely un-intentional. I'm pretty sure that when he used his arms to help me get back my balance, he didn't mean for them to wrap themselves around me. In the dark of the closet I could feel his chin against my temple. We stood that way for what seemed like a lifetime, but at the same time felt as if it could never be long enough. "But it didn't go wrong," he whispered at last. His breath tickled the hair hanging around my ear, and warmed my cheek.

I wanted to relax into him at that moment. I wanted my hands to reach up and grab hold of those shoulders. I wished that I dared to raise my head and . . . well. It didn't matter. I couldn't. "I'm not that type," I was hor-rified to hear myself saying aloud. *Creeeezus!*

"What type?" he murmured, running the sharp edge of his jawline against my forehead. It made me want to melt.

"Uh, you know. The type who gets into trouble at school." My mistake made it easier to regain my senses. Now if only he'd let go of me instead of holding me so close and forcing me to inhale deep lungfuls of his soapy, clean scent. "Gio, I'm *not*."

His fingers smoothed back my hair. Where he had touched me, my skin tingled and danced with an invisible energy that faded much too quickly. I never wanted it to stop. "No one said you were."

"I know, but—"

I felt a finger rest on my lips. "Ssshh." The warmth

disappeared, only to be replaced by warmth of a different kind—softer and moister. His hand gently moved to the back of my neck, encouraging me to accept his kiss.

There was only a phantom of a moment when I wanted to resist. It was impossible not to melt into him and enjoy the sensation of nibbling at each other's lips while our tongues . . . well, did what tongues do. It wasn't my first kiss. Not really, since when I was thirteen Ryan Borville and I had been dared to French kiss while the rest of my seventh-grade class looked on. That was nothing like this. Ryan's tongue had been like a darting eel. Gio was gentle and sweet, and I could easily imagine kissing him in this closet forever and never coming up for air.

I could really learn to enjoy kissing if it was like this. Oh, hey, I didn't want to swap spit with *anyone*—only with Gio. It didn't make me a slut because I really, really liked it, did it? Because I wasn't. I could stop anytime I wanted. Trouble is, I didn't want to.

"Of course you're not," said Gio. It actually hurt that he pulled his lips away from my neck, even for a few seconds.

"Not what?" I whispered back.

"Of course you're not a slut." Oh, salami turds! Was I talking aloud again? "I wouldn't be kissing you if you were."

That was a compliment, right? It didn't mean I'd only get further than kissing if I *was* a slut? I suppose I have a suspicious nature. I really don't know much about getting along with boys. While my hands wanted to grab him and my lips wanted to take a guided tour all over his face, part of me still wanted to run. Why did he frighten me? He'd never given me a single reason to distrust him.

I could see his face now, pale in the gray. We gazed at each other, our eyes like dark pools that reflected light from the hallway. "You're so . . . amazing. I think we make a fantastic couple," he told me.

"You do?" Honestly, I wasn't trying to be all girlie-girlie on him. I hate girls who spend hours in front of their little makeup mirrors and then act all coy and bashful when someone tells them they look good. Gio, however, kept paying me mind-blowing compliments. I knew he thought well of my talent. To know he wanted to cover me with *muchas* smoochies . . . let's just say it was a little overwhelming. I had to know something, though. "Couple? Like in . . . you know. Not only magic?"

"Yes, please." He stretched his mouth wide and smiled, which made me relax enough to reach up and ruffle his hair. It was as soft and silky as I'd always imagined it would be. Touching him like that was only a simple gesture, but to me it was the greatest luxury in the world. "You look so pretty right now."

"Goat," I told him. Then I repeated, "Goat!" While he was talking, I realized why we were suddenly able to see each other's faces: the door to the closet was wide open! My first thought was that someone had pulled it open while we were mashing faces together. During our distraction, though, Rambo had nosed open the door and made a sneak exit.

Gio looked at the door, then back at me. "Oh, crap." He started laughing.

"It's not funny!"

"Okay, okay! Don't worry. We'll get him back." I grabbed his arm as he turned to leave the closet. "What?"

"Maybe we don't want him back. Maybe we leave now and go home and forget about it."

With a cock of his head, he reminded me, "Getting Rambo back to his pen is what makes it a magic trick. Goats don't do that on their own. If we leave, it's going to look like he escaped on his own."

"Maybe that's *good!*" Oh, I didn't know. After kissing him there was nothing I wanted more than to make Gio proud. However, I really didn't want to end the night having to clean out my locker and leave the school district for good. "I don't want the credit anymore!"

"I don't get it. Don't you know what this is going to do for your rep around here?"

"That's what I'm worried about. We could get into *real* trouble if we're caught." We were standing apart now, and from our tones it didn't sound like we were going to be clinching again anytime soon. "I don't want to be a legend."

"I thought you did." He stepped back farther.

Crud. He hated me now. I was cursed to have only two minutes of out-of-this-world kissing in a closet with the boy I most liked in the school—the *only* boy I'd ever liked in any school—and I'd made him my enemy. If I'd gone along with the plan, we'd be smooching still. I sighed. When he reached out and touched my hand, I nearly flinched right out of my skin. "Hey. Come on. We won't do anything you don't want to do. Let's first see if we can find Rambo and get him back to his pen. Then we'll talk. Okay?"

You know those ads on television for indigestion where the guys are clutching their stomachs one minute, and then after they've taken a miracle pill they're totally blissed out and sighing? Yeah. That was me. Times ten.

"Come on." He pulled me out into the hall. "Let's find Rambo."

Since my mom died I've lived in L.A. and Cleveland and Minneapolis and Pittsburgh, and I am here to testify that if I'd been living in any of those other places I would not have been creeping around my high school like some kind of psycho killer. Okay, it's solely because none of those other places even *had* a school mascot as a 4-H project. Still, there's something to be said about big-city schools other than "Aw, man, not *another* weapons search!"

"Okay." The hallway smelled like shavings from the wood shop and sweat from the gym a hundred feet away, but it was a darned sight better than the lethal combination of goat and Clorox. "If I was a goat loose in a high school, where would I go?"

"The art room," Gio answered right away.

"Do you think? I'd probably head for the cafeteria . . . oh." Apparently, goats loose in a high school prefer to be standing about thirty feet down the corridor, chewing on a macramé tassel hanging from the art-room door-knob. Maybe this would be easier than I thought.

We stood there and stared at him for a moment.

Rambo seemed to be giving us the voodoo eyeball while he munched away at the macramé. "Don't . . . make any . . . sudden moves . . ." Gio suggested. He started inching down the hallway in slow motion with his hands stretched out to the sides, like an astronaut on the moon. "Sssssh, keep the noise low. Nice Rambo!" he suggested.

Rambo's expression seemed more like *The heck you say!* than *Hey, thanks!* but he kept still. "Nice Rambo!" I repeated.

That did it. Rambo took one look at me, huffed what sounded like some kind of barnyard curse through his nostrils, and scurried around the corner as fast as his hooves could take him.

"I *knew* that goat hated me!" I said. "All he does is eat and sleep, my aunt Fanny!"

"Um." Gio made a face. "Maybe you'd better not talk to him."

Off we ran around the corner to the long hallway that bisected the school's upper and lower halves. The goat had paused to grab a mouthful of a beaded wall-hanging made by some ancient generation of Fillmore art students. I mean, that ugly thing was positively prehistoric. If you lifted it, you'd probably find cave paintings underneath. Both Gio and I skidded to a stop when we saw him, but Rambo was already off and running again.

Although the wall hanging looked like some kind of six-foot-long torture-chamber abacus, its big brown wooden beads must have held some kind of goat appeal. Rambo had grabbed on to the bottom knob with his teeth and wouldn't let go. When it snagged on the screw pinning it up, he kept hanging on as he scrambled away. Another tug, and the rope broke in half. Wooden beads the size of jumbo grapes began to cascade from the broken cord as Rambo scrambled toward the auditorium. They all clattered and rolled as they tumbled from the strings, and then bounced back into life every time we kicked them. There have been a few times I've been to the movies and someone in the upper rows has dropped their box of M&Ms and the little candies bounced their way down the cement to the levels below. This was pretty much the same, only about a hundred times louder, and those beads weren't made to melt in my mouth.

"Be careful!" Gio warned me, a couple of times reaching out for my hand when it looked as if I might stumble. Then, "Ooof!" Famous last words. He went down, hard, on his knees. A half dozen beads scattered and bounced against the wall.

I stuck out a hand to help him up, but he shook his head. "Get the goat," he growled.

He caught up to me halfway to the auditorium. Beads were still flying off the hanging one by one—larger projectiles now, the size of small oranges. Mostly they were easy to avoid, but when one hit my shin I nearly yelled in pain. That was going to leave a nasty bruise.

Rambo was really booking by this time. He didn't even look behind him as he ran, his ears flattened against his head. Without warning, he swerved and took the far corridor that ran up to the front of the school. Beads kept bouncing down the auditorium corridor and smashing into the wall.

95

We turned and followed. Avoiding the slippery beads on the floor was making us lose ground—and against an animal whose only uses were making cheese and other goats! There was a light on in the yearbook office, but the whole front half of the school had its hallway lights on. Only the deaf could avoid noticing the volley of beads scattering everywhere. No one was supposed to be in this part of the school at this time of night, but I kept cringing at the thought of a custodian or someone else stepping out from one of the classrooms and catching us.

I really did not want to be there. If it hadn't been for Gio doggedly running on, I would've beelined for a door and hightailed it home. "Follow the goat!" he ordered me, when near the front of the building Rambo made a sudden left turn and vanished down the little hallway where the foreign-language labs sat. "I'll go around the other way and head—"

I assumed he meant he was going to head it off, but he'd vanished down the other corridor by then. I'm not the kind of girl who prays a lot, but I found myself composing a letter to heaven in my head as I ran on. I was out of breath and tired and wanted to cry, so mostly it came out as, *Please please please please PLEASE please please please*. You couldn't discount its sincerity, though.

Rambo paused slightly when he reached the junction of corridors. I saw him swing his head in both directions. All the large and medium-size beads at the top of the hanging had scattered behind us at that point. All that was left were a few hundred pea-size spheres of wood, several yards-long fragments of straggly twine, and the large knob in his mouth. Then he scrabbled toward the main office and disappeared.

Outside the front windows of the school, everything looked nice and normal, the way I wished my life was, most of the time. Why did I have to get cursed with all the freaky bad luck? I bet the people in the houses across the streets were nice and happy and eating their late dinners and watching TV and knitting and doing the sorts of things that normal, upstanding— Hey, wait. Was there someone behind me? I turned, thinking for a minute that maybe Rambo had doubled around somehow and was running up toward the back of the school again. But there was nothing except the trail of beads we'd left behind, and the school's front hallway ahead. Creepy. I could've sworn I'd heard something.

At least Rambo had avoided toppling the bust of Millard Fillmore, I thought to myself when I crept forward. "Whoa!" Something grabbed my arm.

It was Gio. His head swiveled back and forth the way it might if he were watching a Ping-Pong tournament with the fast-forward button pressed. "Where'd he go?" he asked. "Are you okay?"

Standing there in a section of the school off-limits to us at that time of night, surrounded by hundreds of tiny wooden beads spread by a goat we'd liberated for a prank of our own gone horribly wrong, I thought it was sweet that he was concerned about me. I had more sense than to gush, though. "I'm fine. He went your way. Didn't you see him?"

"No, I came around the corner and saw you. . . ." Gio's

words faded while we both looked at the floor. We both realized we could track Rambo easily; all we had to do was follow the trail of beads. It led to a front office door, which stood half-open, as if something had pushed its way in.

"We are going to get into *so* much trouble if we get caught in there." I felt as if I'd swallowed a whole baby alligator and it was trying to eat its way out of my stomach one chomp at a time.

"I think at this point we're in trouble regardless," Gio pointed out.

"We could still get the heck out of Dodge!"

"He'll be cornered in there, though. An easy catch. I say we get him, take him to his pen, and *then* we can go. We can still salvage this!" Gio attempted to shift his weight, but he slipped on several of the beads still decorating the floor. He overbalanced and fell backward . . . right onto the pedestal holding Fillmore's plaster statue.

"No!" I cried. It was one of those moments in which time seemed to slow down. My brain flashed into overdrive so I could see every little thing that happened. The bump against the pedestal only jarred it a little and set the statue wobbling. My muscles relaxed for a split second. Then, when Gio scrabbled for a handhold, his fingers clawed against the pedestal and tipped it slightly. The bust toppled sideways.

You've got to have good reflexes to pull off magic stunts. Although the beads were treacherous underfoot, I dove forward and held out my hands to catch the statue. It was heavier than I thought. Lots heavier. "Oof!" I remember yelling. I said something much worse when I stumbled and banged the statue, hard, against the still-wobbling wooden pedestal. Had I damaged it? I saw with alarm that I'd whacked poor Millard somewhere in the face.

"Oh, sheesh, I'm sorry," Gio said over my shoulder. "Great catch, though. Is it okay?"

"I think so," I told him. "Help me with it."

Together we settled the thirteenth president of the United States back atop his home. He looked fine. Great, in fact, for someone with such a weird name. "That was close," Gio said with a sigh.

"No kidding." I felt cold goose bumps rise on the back of my neck once again. "Did you hear something?" I asked.

Gio looked around and shook his head. "Maybe, but there's no one here." For a second we stood there looking at ol' Millard, proud of our close call. Maybe everything was going to be okay, after all.

Plink. Millard's nose fell from his face and onto the floor, where it cracked into two large pieces and a considerable amount of powder.

Some days you can't get a break.

I looked at the plaster and dust on the floor. That nose was the last straw. I felt personally affronted by that nose. That nose seemed to be spitting at me. Not literally. That would be kind of gross. Metaphorically. Mr. Iverson is always going on and on in English class about how objects become symbols and metaphors for other things. That nose lying on the floor represented everything the exact opposite of what I had wanted from this evening. It was like Millard Fillmore himself giving me the big bird. And you know what? I wasn't going to take that from some guy whose mother named him after a duck.

No, wait. That's *mallard*. Well, whatever.

"We're going in to get that goat," I told Gio. I wasn't going to take any backtalk. Take-charge, tough Vick was in the building! "Come on. Follow me."

I think Gio liked take-charge Vick. He kind of grinned, nodded, and let me assume the lead.

Rambo must have gotten tired of the former wall hanging after all the beads had trickled off, because right as we crept into the main office, we stepped over the remains of the cords and the gnawed-on knob that used to hang from the bottom. Some of the secretary's office supplies obviously seemed to have goat appeal; I was particularly disgusted by a stapler that Rambo had snagged from Mrs. Detweiler's cubicle and left all slobbery on the floor. Oh, yeah, Rambo had definitely been there. You could smell goat everywhere. There was another stink too that I couldn't quite identify at first. It was faint, and barely tickling at my nostrils.

The overhead lights were set at dim. All the back offices were dark except one, and it was from its direction that I heard the noise of desk supplies falling to the floor. "This way." Gio crept behind me. "Maybe you'd better let me do the talking when we get there," he reminded me.

"Oh, no," I told him. "No way. I've got quite a few words I want to say to that goat." As if he heard me coming, Rambo bleated pitifully from the office. "Stay here," I told Gio. He pressed himself against the back wall. I held my breath and leaped over to the doorway and took a look.

And a whiff. "Bleaugh!" I choked out, pulling the door shut to make it stop. Light from the hallway accented the brass nameplate on the door as it swung closed: VICE PRINCIPAL HOWARD V. DERMOT. My hand was still over my mouth and nose when I tiptoed back to Gio.

"Rambo in there?"

"Oh, yeah," I said. "Is he ever. You remember last year when those seniors from the football team left a diaper of Rambo poo in Dermot's office?"

"Yeah . . ." Gio said, looking absolutely horrified.

"Cut to this year. Similar situation, no diaper."

"Oh, sh—"

"What the . . . !" Even with the front office doors shut, we could hear the shouting from outside. The screeching's volume tripled the closer it came to the door. *"Vandalism! Hooliganism!* Right under my own *nose!"*

It was like one of those sounds in the movies that the military develops in secret to kill people from a distance, but I didn't have time to throw my hands over my ears or chomp down on the cyanide pill in my hollow tooth, because Gio was tugging on my wrist. We dropped to our hands and knees and crawled along the floor to the far side of the secretary's cube as quickly as we could. The high cubicle walls would protect us, or so I hoped. I said a short prayer of thanks for Gio's quick thinking. When I'd heard the Doormat fishing for his keys, all I could do was freeze and think of was how sad my dad would be when I told him we were going to have to move because I'd been banned from all the public and private schools in the state for letting a goat do his doody all over the vice principal's office.

"This is *outrageous,*" muttered the vice principal as he stormed in. I heard him pause by the long front desk. ". . . calling the police! These kids aren't getting away with murder. Not on Howard Dermot's watch."

I looked at Gio, totally alarmed. *The police?* I mouthed at him. Take-charge Vick had left the building!

He held a finger to his lips, then put his other hand on top of mine to comfort me. I tried not to panic, I really did, but with every punch of the buttons I was one number closer to being the youngest goatnapper in the big house.

A terrible crash sounded from behind the closed office door. It sounded as if Rambo, tired of being cooped up with no macramé munchies, had pulled over one of the bookcases. Gio bit his lip and squeezed up his face until it was wrinkly. He looked as frightened as I did, but I could tell he was trying not to laugh—not because he thought this situation was hilarious, but because there really wasn't any other way to react that didn't involve leaving streaks on our underwear. Once I saw the laughter on his face, I couldn't help it. I wanted to laugh myself. This was ridiculous. This entire evening seemed unreal. Especially when we had kissed. Maybe I'd dreamed up that part.

I sucked in my lips and stayed quiet. "What was that?"

Dermot said. I heard him replace the phone in the cradle. Then, in a hiss, "Who's in my office?"

Gio leaned over and put his mouth against my ear. His words were deadly quiet, but his breath was hot against my lobe and neck as he whispered, "Remember that plan of yours earlier about skedaddling?"

I nodded.

He nodded.

Crawling quickly on our hands and knees, we reached the office door right as the vice principal opened his. I heard gagging noises. A goat bleating. Silence.

And then: "I'm going to kill the hoodlums who did this!"

It wasn't until we had made it out the front door, flew over the front lawn, crossed the street, and ran a block south of the school grounds that we dared to look over our shoulders. No one followed, but I half expected to hear the police sirens at any moment. "I don't know about you," Gio said, as out of breath as I was, "but I think it might be best if we split up from here."

" 'Bye," I said by way of agreement.

" 'Bye. Oh!" He grabbed my wrist before I could run off in the opposite direction. I thought he was going to tell me to be careful, or to thank me, or something, but instead he took the back of my head and pulled me to him. His lips met mine, and I found myself sinking into another kiss. "I'll call you tomorrow," he whispered. Then he grinned, winked, and ran off. His long shadow sliced through pools of lamplight until at last he jogged across the street and disappeared.

So the kissing part *had* been real, after all!

CHAPTER EIGHT

I guess it would be fair to say relations between Addy and me had been kind of cold since that afternoon at Arcadia Mall. You know, the kind of cold you get when it's the hottest afternoon of the summer and you've been outside in the sun all day working up a sweat and then you plunge into a convenience store where the air conditioner's working overtime and you head right for the Slurpee machine because it looks so good and frosty and you fill up your sixty-four-ounce cup with a mixture of frozen cola and watermelon and stick two straws in it and suck up a glorious mouthful of ice crystals that go straight to your sinuses and give you a crushing case of brain freeze and a headache that makes you wish you were never born. Yeah, that kind of cold, right down to the blinding, floor-pounding headache.

In fact, we hadn't spoken a word in a week. Addy avoided sitting at the losers' table during lunch, and Ray and Des and Dorie didn't know where she was—or they wouldn't tell me. In English and science, where the teachers had an open seating plan, she would come in at the last possible moment and sit on the opposite side of the room. In geometry, where McClenny made us take the same seats every time, she sat with her hands on her desk, face forward, her new hair obscuring her face from me. She never once looked in my direction. After class she would become involved with her bookbag and never raise her head until I left the room.

I didn't press her to be friends again, admittedly. I know—my fault. But I figured if she was going to be in a snit over something minor like me leaving her alone for two whole minutes, she could get over it already. That's baby stuff, like a Hello Kitty lunchbox. Who needs that?

I did.

After the Friday-night fiasco I needed Addy more than ever. When I got home that evening I wanted nothing more than to call her up on the phone, crawl under the covers, and talk like we used to, until we were both yawning so hard our mouths could've sucked in bugs from fifty feet away. More than that, I wanted to tell her everything. And I do mean *everything*, from the big lie I could never reveal to the Incredible Disappearing Rambo the Killer Mountain Goat disaster. More than anything in the world I wanted to hear her say that it was okay and that she liked me anyway.

I wanted to tell her the good stuff, too. I could have shared with her what happened in the closet, and how it felt to kiss a boy. She would have enjoyed hearing about that, I think.

Instead, I got silence. And that was exactly what I gave back. Obviously one of us was going to have to apologize. For the previous week I had thought it should be up to Addy. Now I wasn't so sure.

I arranged to bump into her Monday morning. I knew Mrs. Kornwolf dropped her off at the side entrance in the mornings, but if Addy saw me lurking on the steps, she might get her mom to pull around somewhere else. So I lingered inside the door and timed it so I happened to be wandering out the door when Addy's sandals hit the sidewalk. "Oh, hey!" I said, like it was a big surprise.

She had already started to cross the grass in a direction away from me—toward Bart Nelson, of all people. He stood there watching her with a cocky grin on his face. All my instincts to protect Addy leaped into play. "Hey," I said more loudly, when I got close enough to grab her jacket.

She stopped and gave Bart a look when I tugged at her sleeve. I'd assumed she hadn't noticed the skeezer lying in wait for her. From the glance she gave him, though, it almost seemed as if she'd rather have a run-in with Bart than with me. Hadn't she learned anything from her Pop Alley incident earlier that month? You stick to people who have your best interests at heart, every time! She stood there passively and looked down at the ground, refusing to meet my eyes. "Hello." She shifted the papers in her arms.

Time to get things back on an old familiar footing. "Whatcha got there?" From inside the school I'd noticed her inspecting the file folder on top of her stack, obviously checking to see if something important was safe. When I'd seen the thin pile of white typing paper inside, I had dug into my own bag and gotten a stunt ready. Addy loved this trick.

"My history proj— Don't!" She squealed when I grabbed the contents from their folder. The infamous history paper, word-processed so neatly. My back was close to the wall; no one could tell that when I pretended to be passing off Addy's project from hand to hand behind my back, I'd be switching it with the dummy pages inside my jacket. "It's due today. This isn't funny!" she snapped.

I made the switch and kept on passing off the paper between my hands, taunting her by holding it out of reach. "C'mon, be a rainbow, not a pain-bow," I urged her with a grin. How many times had she seen me magically restore ripped-up notes and papers? I'd have her playing along soon. Things would be exactly like they used to be. "Want to do something after school?"

"No." She made a feint to retrieve the paper, but I was too quick for her. I almost felt guilty at her desperation. Behind her pretty new hair and her pretty new clothes, Addy was still the same old girl wearing the same red-cheeked, tight-lipped look that signaled approaching tears. "Just give it *back*."

I would've torn the dummy pages and restored the real thing right there if Bart Nelson hadn't stuck his nose into things. "Marotti, why don't you give the girl her paper?"

"Why, so you can copy off it, brainiac?" I didn't need his kind to be telling me what to do. He stared at me for a second, his jaw slack. Some people seem to get a lot of pleasure out of hauling off and decking someone. Me, I like to get in my punches verbally. I felt good about making him speechless. I pulled down my mouth and made an imitation of his face. "Duuuhh!"

He blinked. "You're out of control, Marotti. Give the lady back her paper."

Had I made the switch? I'd lost track during the argument. I passed my right hand with the paper behind my back. My left hand came around with the dummy pages. "Listen, Nelson, I've got a a little suggestion that I'll spell out for you in simple words. Why don't you go to the bank, sit down, fill out a form for a small loan, and start your *own* business, okay? Because you've got no right getting into *mine*. So, like, shoo."

I grinned at Addy, knowing she'd be grateful I'd stuck up for her. Then I ripped her history project in half.

I knew something was wrong immediately after the first rip. Addy was supposed to see the blank dummy pages and think they were the backs of her printed project. Right after I made a long tear down the paper in my hands, some part of my brain realized that what I'd just shredded was covered with words. Before the thought fully processed, I'd torn the paper into quarters.

I halted. Addy stood there with her arms crossed. It didn't take an English-Sulky/Sulky-English dictionary to see that she had *Go on, get it over with already* written all over her face. I thought over what I'd done in the minutes before. Was it possible I'd made the switch twice? Holy hell! It was the only explanation . . . but I never made mistakes like that. At least, I never used to.

I stood there, absolutely horrified. The bits of paper in my hand felt like they burned my skin. The fire spread up my arms and across my neck and scalp and down my chest, paralyzing me and making breathing impossible. I guessed it was probably unlikely that lightning would strike me right then. I thought about my other options. I could run into the school. I could burst into tears. Or I could own up.

The last was as simple as opening my hands, but it was also the hardest thing I've ever done. I felt like my windpipe was about as wide as a No. 2 pencil. "I'm sorry," I choked. My hands trembled as I held out the shreds. I still held out hope I'd be ground zero for a meteor strike at that moment.

Bart broke the silence. "Jesus, Marotti. Why'd you do that?"

It was funny. All around us people were walking by, talking, going through the early-morning motions, and I couldn't hear a thing except my own ragged breathing. I was totally fixated on Addy's reaction. Would she cry? Would she scream? Would she slap me? Would she go postal?

She didn't do any of those things. She stared at the pieces of her history paper, then looked at me with no trace of expression. That was worse than crying. After a long, long moment, she finally snatched the shreds from my hands and stuck them back into the folder.

"I'm sorry," I repeated. "Maybe we could get some tape. . . ."

"She doesn't want your help." Bart held me at a distance so I couldn't get any closer to her.

"Get *away* from Addy!"

Addy reached out and grabbed Bart's hand. "No, Vick. Get away from *me*. Get away from *us*." The look on her face was hostile. It was challenging. It was the look of someone who knew she was in the right. "And you know what? *Stay* away."

"But—"

That was when I noticed they were still holding hands. Together they stalked off toward the school's front lawn. Bart looked at me over his shoulder as they went, then shook his head like I was the lowest thing on earth. She didn't glance back once. "It's okay, baby," I heard him say.

"It's on the computer at home. But it's due today!"

"Your mom can print out another copy and bring it. Just tell the teacher what happened and . . ."

As they got too far away for me to hear, I finally put it all together. The hands. The way he had been hanging around. His use of the word *baby*.

Addy and Bart were . . . Oh, God, I couldn't think the words to myself. *Dating?* Getting groinal? Whatever! Ewww! I didn't know what she thought she was doing. The realization that my best friend was doing the snuggly with the person I'd most like to see afflicted with Ebola hit me like a Looney Tunes anvil dropped on my head from the top of a cliff. She chose *him* over me? How dare she!

My anger vanished momentarily when I flashed back

to the shredded paper in my hands. I had ruined the history project she'd worked on for weeks! Maybe I didn't deserve any friends, I thought to myself in my shame, as I staggered into the school. It's not like I treated them well. I hadn't been around for any member of my little losers' club for the past couple of weeks, and it was obvious that Addy had been lonely enough to fall into the arms of the first sleazy, leering . . .

No wonder she had changed her hair. Now it was all starting to make sense, I realized. Someone knocked into me as I started up the steps to the outside door, but I was so lost in thought I didn't even remember to snarl. She hadn't glammed up for herself. She'd done it for a stupid *boy*. Of all the idiotic things! You didn't change yourself against your better judgment to please a boy!

You did, Friday, I reminded myself. The thought made the same empty, lonely sound as a pebble dropped into an old well.

That was different. My situation was . . . Wait. Hold on! I grabbed onto the rail as I turned at the top of the landing. I had another flashback to the day I'd laid the voodoo whammy on Bart when I'd caught him picking on Addy in Pop Alley. The memory of Addy's face that day, flushed and embarrassed, seemed to hover over me like that scene in the movie when Oz the Great and Terrible appears before Dorothy and her friends. Only not so green.

She and Bart hadn't been fighting at all that afternoon. I'd burst onto the scene and assumed he was picking on her. I remembered the way he was holding her against

111

the pop machine, her red face, his leer. My brain had taken all that visual information and interpreted it as bullying—but the only danger Addy had been in that day was of getting a serious hickey!

I felt my face getting hot well before I realized how enraged I was. That little snake! She had been sneaking around with Bart before I'd *met* Gio! And she hadn't told me!

I couldn't believe Addy Kornwolf, my best friend in the entire world, had been keeping secrets from me! Not any old secret, either. As far as secrets went, this one made a great humpbacked whale seem about as massive as a termite. She'd been lying to me for weeks. Was I supposed to watch her stroll off with the sleaziest mouth-breather ever to crawl out from some pool of Jurassic slime?

Well, screw that!

"Uh, sorry!" Some thin redheaded geek collided with me as he jumped down the stairs two at a time onto the sidewalk. "Didn't mean to."

"Watch where you're going, freak!" With both hands I reached out and pushed the guy on his chest. Hard. He sprawled backward onto his butt, but his oversize backpack cushioned him from landing too hard. A bunch of papers and books spilled from the top.

I instantly felt miserable at what I'd done. There had been a look of genuine fear in the kid's eyes when I'd grabbed and shoved him. At the other schools where I'd been bullied a long time ago, I'd looked like that. I lived in fear, back then, that some random psycho would rough me up merely for walking by. And here I was, the randomest psycho around. "Crap," I said, feeling like the wadded-up paper towel someone's used to wipe dog poop from his boot. "I'm sorry."

The geek scrambled away when I knelt down to help him retrieve his books. "I probably deserved it," he said.

That got me angry. "No, goofus, you didn't. You Kick-Mes make me sick. *No one* deserves to be treated that way." It was stupid, me venting at this guy. My anger had nothing to do with him. It was Addy I despised, and all her lies.

What about the lie you've lived all year?

The thought cut through me like an icy knife. I didn't want to think about that, though. Not now. That was entirely different from Addy's betrayal. Entirely different!

I was scraping up the last of the kid's mess—honestly, I don't know how much of that Dungeons & Dragons stuff a single guy needs during school hours, but whatever—when I felt a tap on my shoulder. "What the—" I started to snarl while I pivoted to look over my shoulder.

Vice Principal Dermot stood over me. The look on his face would've soured marshmallow Peeps.

It was one of those moments where even Calgon can't take you away. My brain started working on overdrive. Had he seen me push the neutral good geekazoid wielding the +5 Acne Wipes of Power? Was it because of Addy's paper? Had she ratted on me? Another possibility loomed, more ominous than those combined, but I didn't want to think about it. The old noggin was processing so many potential pitfalls that it simply shorted out on me. "I didn't . . ." I stammered out. "I mean, I wasn't . . ."

The Doormat had a wince of pain on his face as he addressed D&D boy. "Perkins, stop being such an oaf and get your act together," he said. "Get to class."

For a second I was outraged on Perkins's behalf. The accident hadn't been his fault at all! Since I wasn't in one of those self-sacrificing, "far, far better thing I do today" Sydney Carlton moods, though, I handed the kid the rest of his dungeon maps and tried smiling at him. He fled without a thank you, but who can blame him?

"You," announced Dermot, grabbing me by the collar, "are coming with me."

He practically dragged me around the corner. Kids parted to make way for us. Next thing I knew, he'd turned the knob of a door I'd never noticed before and hustled me inside. No wonder I'd never noticed the door; it was to a staff lounge. Two dozen teachers were hanging around inside, drinking coffee and talking before the first bell, but when we burst in, all the chatter dropped to a hush I haven't heard since I was seven and let out a ripe belch in church. They seemed surprised to see the vice principal, but were more surprised that a student had ventured into their off-limits lair.

I didn't get much of an opportunity to apologize. Dermot maneuvered me to a chair covered with ratty upholstery and thrust me down. He leaned on the chair's arms and hovered. If his eyes had bored into me any more intently, they would've gone straight through my skull and to the center of the earth. "I want to know exactly what you had to do with it," he growled at me.

"With what?" I didn't have to pretend confusion. I had

so much to do with so many things that I didn't know which "it" he meant.

He screwed up his eyes and glared. "I understand from several members of the football team that you made threats against them Friday afternoon." Okay, so it was that. I couldn't do more than shrug. I didn't mind being accused of the threat. It was what came after that I worried about.

Though my exterior was cool, my insides experienced nuclear meltdown. Dermot's breath was as rank as ever. I felt my nose hairs curl and burn as he leaned in farther to inquire, "Is there anything else you'd like to tell me?"

If my life had been an after-school special, I would have blabbed it all and learned a very special lesson about Doing the Right Thing for the Right Reasons. I'd done a very bad thing for very bad reasons, though. Worse, Gio was involved. There was no way on earth I could deliberately get Gio into trouble. He was one of those kids with a bright future ahead of him, and I . . . well. I was just me. It's hard to see a future when the day-to-day is so bad. I had to say something. I discarded "Ever considered waxing? You're putting the 'o-no!' in 'monobrow' there, mister!" as too flippant, and stuck with, "I don't understand."

"Oh, I think you *do*." He glared at me. "I think you *do*!" As he continued to hover there, not moving, I realized something: he didn't know anything at all about who was behind the Rambo incident. He was grasping at straws and hoping I'd cave in. Sure, the guys from the team might have tattled on my threat, but what's that worth? I didn't specifically mention goats, not ever. They came up with that connection themselves.

Okay, so that's what we knew they'd do. But suspicions still didn't add up to hard evidence. Besides, these were the same guys who'd pulled a similar stunt last year. I decided to brazen it out. "I'm sorry I threatened the football players?" I asked, as if hoping that was the response he wanted. "It's not like I could beat them up or anything," I added, with some eye rolling for dramatic effect.

I was beginning to think that Dermot was going to give me the bad cop treatment for the rest of the day. Finally Mr. Iverson, my English teacher, came over. "Mr. Dermot," he murmured politely, "with the greatest respect, I don't believe this is either the time or place. As Miss Marotti's first period teacher, may I assure you I shall escort her directly to class?"

Good old tweedy Iverson! I swore right then I would never complain about subtext or irony or the *Canterbury Tales* ever again. The Doormat pursed his lips, obviously thwarted. I let Mr. Iverson help me up from the chair and glide me past the rest of the shocked teachers. From their expressions, they didn't seem too fond of the vice principal. In fact I could've sworn that Iverson muttered the words "self-righteous jerk" as we stepped into the hallway, but it might have been my imagination. I kind of hoped it wasn't.

Before we were able to take more than two steps, the door opened again behind us. "Hold it, Iverson," said the vice principal. He swung around to confront me again and stared me in the eyes. "If I get any evidence you had *anything* to do with the goings-on Friday night, you're out of here. Out. No appeals, no defense. O-U-T. Do I make myself clear?" I didn't dignify the threat with an answer. I tried to look confused, but Dermot was too busy narrowing his eyes and pointing first at them and then at me. I guess it meant he was going to be watching me. Either that or he wanted to borrow some Visine.

Crap. Crap. Crap!

Addy never showed up for math. I sat next to her empty chair and felt like the worst person in the world. Maybe I was. I didn't bother to visit the cafeteria for lunch. Des and the others would side with Addy, plain and simple. No matter how much I'd done for them over the last year, they were going to think I'd crossed the line. It was pretty plain that the only person I could turn to at this point would be Gio. And during school hours I had to pretend I didn't like him.

I wanted to wake up back home in my bed and find that the entire day—the entire month!—had been one long bad dream. I had only one consolation: at least I knew the day couldn't get worse.

Before my last period, I stopped off at my locker to pick up my stuff to carry home. Everyone around me was laughing and acting like the world hadn't come to an end while I twiddled out the combination. The happy noise bugged me. I kept telling myself that the day would be over soon, and then I could go over to Gio's so we could talk about what to do. I was going to have to be firm with him about any more super-stunts. The misery wasn't worth it. Maybe, I thought to myself, just maybe I should give up the magic thing altogether. There were only a couple more months left in the school year. How many times could I get beaten up in a couple of months?

A lot, unfortunately.

When I swung open my locker, a couple of things fell from the top of the door, as if they'd been shoved through the crack at the top. One was a manila envelope, the other a folded sticky note. I unfolded the smaller note and read it.

V.—

Hey! Couldn't reach you this weekend. What up?
Call me when you get home. Can't see you tonight.
I told my folks I'd go through some college catalogs
with them. Miss you.
—G.

Down the tubes went my plans for consolation. Oh, I'd been hoping for some more of the kissing action, no doubt. But mostly I wanted to pour my heart out to Gio. I knew he'd understand how miserable the day had been for me. What was in the envelope, though? Had he printed out some more Internet articles on Houdini?

I opened the envelope's flap. Inside sat a half dozen black and white photographs. They were slightly fuzzy, like photos taken from far away and enlarged to pick out a detail. Yet they were all clear enough to see the main subject: me.

Every droplet of blood drained from my head as I

flipped through the glossies. There was my back, running down the hallway toward the front of the school with beads everywhere. There was a side shot of me looking out the front windows of the school. There was me, diving at the bust of Millard Fillmore—only it really looked like I was *trying* to knock it over. Gio was in that photo, too, but his face was blocked out by my hands. His leg appeared in the photo of us entering the main office, but there I was, clear as day. I was apparently also having a photogenic moment when we crawled back out of the office, but once again I was blotting out any trace of Gio.

There was a note with the photos. I didn't recognize the handwriting.

Gotcha.

Chapter Nine

"Oh . . . Vick." Gio's mom had opened her front door with a bit of an irritated expression. I could hardly blame her, the way I'd been punching at the doorbell like a possessed Avon lady who'd knocked back way too much caffeine. I couldn't help but notice that her grim smile managed to fade a little when she saw me blackening the front stoop. "What a surprise!" The gritted teeth might have been my imagination, but from the way she blocked the door it didn't take psychic powers to tell me I wasn't exactly welcome. "We're having dinner."

Since I could see past her to the dining room and could hear forks against plates, I knew she wasn't just trying to get rid of me. "I know I must seem like the rudest person in the world to show up unannounced during your family's dinner, Mrs. Carson," I said in my most sincere and polite voice, hoping that I wasn't coming off all Eddie Haskell when I really meant every word, "but can I speak to Gio really quickly for a minute? I won't do it again."

While she mulled over my bargain, I added, "*Ever*. It's really urgent. Please?"

I guess the politeness worked, because she softened and actually smiled at me ever so slightly. I hadn't been exaggerating. It *was* urgent. After I'd found those photographs in my locker, I felt like an animal trapped in a cage, too panicked to find a route out. Oh, I'd caught enough episodes of afternoon soaps to know what black-mail was all about. I wasn't that naïve. If whoever took those photos were to give them to the Doormat . . . well, I might as well have dropped out of school right then and made my way over to the golden arches for a job appli-cation, because I was going to be spending the rest of my life behind their counter asking, "You want fries with that?" If I was lucky, anyway, and my dad didn't send me to boot camp first.

Man, my life was so *different* from Gio's, I thought to myself as I sat down in his family's living room. In his house it was almost impossible to concentrate on how upset I felt. Everything was so clean and quiet that it felt more like a church. University catalogs sat stacked neatly on the antique coffee table, not one out of alignment, ready for the big college talk later in the evening. North-western. University of Michigan. Brown. The students on their covers looked so *normal*. The camera had caught them smiling and laughing or looking as if they were having deep conversations about, I don't know, French literary theory. I would have given anything to have traded places with them right at that moment.

For some reason I'd always been awed that the Carsons' greeny furniture actually formed a matched set. That whole concept was so alien to me; my dad's few pieces of fake-wood furniture was stuff we'd screwed together ourselves and carted around from city to city in a rental van. The Carsons ate their dinners sitting around a table—all at the same time!—with real silverware and plates and napkins. My meals were mostly Thai takeout I ate in front of the TV, straight out of the box, usually with my fingers. I'd sample it again late at night when my dad would get home from work and eat his portion cold while we caught up on the day together. I loved that, but it wasn't hamburger casserole/mashed potatoes/ grace before dinner *normal*.

Time after time I seemed to get the short end of the good-luck stick. Why was it always *me* who had to be caught with my panties around my ankles when the Porta Potti door flew open? Where was my greeny furniture and my silverware? Where were my college catalogs? I mean, Gio's face hadn't ended up in any of the blackmail photos! How did he get all the good fortune?

". . . quick, please. I don't want this to become a habit."

"It won't. Thanks, Mom," I heard Gio promise. I pulled myself up from a slouch when I heard his voice. "A couple of minutes at most."

"Your beets will get cold." Beets. Even the food they ate was all wholesome and *Father Knows Best*.

I heard footsteps on the hallway carpet, and then Gio was in the room, smiling. His brown eyes were lit up with excitement. He was genuinely happy to see me. In less than thirty words and with only a few photos, I was going to be knocking that beautiful smile right off of his face.

"Hi," he said, stuffing his hands in his pockets. Didn't he trust his hands? Did he want to hold me? I hoped so. "I tried calling you this weekend. I guess you were busy or something."

"Something like that." All weekend I'd avoided answering the phone. As much as I wanted to yum down on Gio's lips and feel his arms around me, my sudden status as a juvenile delinquent and amateur vandal kept me lying low. Now that I was with him once again, I wanted nothing more than to let him comfort me. I couldn't, though. Not with his parents across the hall. Not with so little time. "I have to tell you something."

"What's up? Hey, did you know everyone's talking about Rambo? They think someone let him out before the photo shoot as a joke—either a team member or one of the yearbook staff."

"Yeah, I kind of wanted to talk about that." I looked away from him and down at the college catalogs. He'd be attending one of those colleges the year after next. I could picture him as one of those smiling catalog kids, some genuinely pretty girl looking up into his eyes.

He'd never get to any college if anyone found out about those photos.

"Okay, shoot," he said.

"It's like this," I told him. I reached for my backpack and unzipped it. My hand fished in to draw out the photos. Something compelled me to stop. "I don't think I can see you anymore."

I honestly hadn't intended to say that.

I pulled my hand out of the backpack and zipped it up, then hugged the pack to myself. I'd decided he was never going to see those photos.

"What?" He spoke the word so low I could barely hear it.

I'd plunged razor-sharp icicles into both our hearts. The expression on Gio's face was so blank that I couldn't look at him. During that second when the words hung there in the air between us, though, the decision sounded right.

"I can't see you anymore." That was the solution. Getting him involved in blackmail would only drag him down into the muck with me. He was special. Everyone liked Gio. He couldn't afford to get into trouble. Not like I could.

I knew Gio well enough to be sure he'd want to be a knight in shining armor. He'd come up with some grand plan that would land us both into more trouble. I wasn't having any of it. If anyone was going to do any rescuing here, it would be me. That was my *job*. Why was I fooling myself that kissing him in the broom closet meant anything, anyway? It had been wonderful, but I had to put that behind me. There was no way that Gio could be seriously interested in someone like me. He could do way, way better.

Dumping him was for his own protection. How could I make him see that? What could I say now to make things better? He still looked as if I'd knocked the wind from him. Should I give him the *It's not you, it's me* speech? Isn't that what I was supposed to do? I had no clue. All I could do was sneak little glances at him and wish I could soothe his poor, wounded face with my hands.

"Okay," I said, standing up. "See you later." *Smooth, Vick. Real smooth.* I was so appalled with myself that I wanted to run and hide and never come out into the sunlight again.

He looked almost angry. "What is this crap? You can't come in here and . . . Are you *dumping* me? It doesn't make sense! Friday was . . ." He dropped his volume and looked over his shoulder before continuing. "Okay, so everything didn't go as planned Friday, but there were . . . you know . . . parts you liked, right? Right?" I couldn't answer. "This is so *wrong*."

"Nothing went right Friday."

"Houdini had setbacks!"

"Houdini got punched in the stomach and died from it. That was one major setback, all right," I snapped. "Listen, don't make this hard. It's not you, it's—"

"I don't believe you." His whisper was so fierce it made my pulse race. "I don't believe you at all. There's something else going on."

I was close to losing it. I knew that if I met Gio's eyes, I'd probably break out into a bawl and confess everything that was wrong. There was no way I could risk dragging him into this mess. The worst part was having to lie to save him from it.

So I left. I put up all those walls of toughness and apathy I'd built around myself for the last year and hauled my butt out of there. I didn't pay attention to Mrs. Carson standing in the hallway with her arms crossed. I ignored Gio crying out, "Wait! Wait!" behind me, and I didn't turn to see him standing at the door watching me go.

I couldn't risk breaking my heart that way. With every step, all the real magic I'd ever known in the world slowly drained away. Gio had been the first person ever to reach out and see through all my defenses. It didn't matter to him that other people thought I was a loser. I'd trusted him, and I'd had to throw it all away, and I could never tell him the truth why or let him know what a sacrifice it all was.

That evening I didn't even join my dad for our usual late-night spicy Thai noodles and *I Love Lucy*. When I heard his gentle knock at my door, I pretended I was asleep until he went away. After betraying Addy and hurting Gio, skipping out on my dad's dinner was yet another disappointment to add to the Why Vick Is a Big Buttchop list. It took a night of Kleenex therapy and hugging Mrs. Tiggy-Winkle before I finally climbed out of bed the next morning and into my life again.

But you know, you can only kick me around for so long. Okay, it took several years of getting beaten up at new school after new school before I devised the scheme of pretending I was a witch, but I learned from all that bullying. I found out that it's better to be the protector than someone who needs protecting.

There was no way I was going to let some little Ansel Adams Junior with a camera and a telephoto lens back me into a corner. I'd spent enough time in that corner.

I'd have to size up the competition and see what made her tick.

Funny thing, I was pretty sure I knew who she was.

Addy attended geometry class on Tuesday, at least. When she walked in right before the starting bell sounded over the ceiling loudspeakers, she didn't look at me once. Instead, the whole class got to watch as she and Ms. McClenny had a whispered conference with their backs to the room. At one point Addy reached into her backpack and withdrew a folded piece of paper; the teacher read it, murmured something, and looked around the room. Only briefly did McClenny's eyes flicker on me. The class might have been sleepy, but we're not stupid. Everyone knew something was up.

A second later McClenny pointed to Brian Reed, a kid who sat next to the windows. Five seconds after that I had Brian as a new neighbor, while Addy sat down with a fantastic view of trash bags oozing rancid milk by the cafeteria Dumpster. Brian sat down in his seat in a huff, gave me a look, rolled his eyes, and slouched down. "Maaaaan!" he complained.

"I may not be Captain Hook, but trust me, I can tell you're no treasure either," I snapped back.

Over my left shoulder I heard twin giggles. "Daaaaang," drawled Melinda softly, while the rest of the class chattered at the change. "Someone must've done something *really* wrong."

"No kidding," Brie answered back in the same phony voice.

"Brie, is that your homework? Should I rip it up for you?"

"Oh, would you? I hear you're so *good* at it."

Addy wasn't so far away that she could avoid over-hearing their stupid little game. She kept staring straight ahead, white as a sheet. "Of course I would. I'm a total freaky loser with nothing better to do." Miranda continued their fake conversation.

"Shut up," I whispered to myself. I wanted McClenny to start class. Anything to get them to stop wagging their evil little lipsticked mouths.

"Of course you're not," Brie said. "If you were like, a *total* freaky loser, you wouldn't have *any* friends. Oh, wait. You don't!"

I whipped around. "Stop that."

Brie cocked her head. "Gonna make me?"

"Listen, Cheese Nips," I snarled. "Your little mozzarella butt might be new around these parts, but you can bet you don't know Monterey Jack about half the shiznitz I can call down on you." I really got into mocking her. Every time I brought up a new cheese, Brie's face turned redder and redder. I loved every second of making her squirm. "So you can sit your little Camembert back *down* because I'm Gouda tired of you."

A lot of the kids around me, Brian included, giggled at Brie's embarrassment. I might be the one they usually ragged on, but none of them ever gave up the chance to get in a good laugh at someone made weak. When Brie finally looked back up at me, I could tell by the steel in her eyes that at that moment she hated me more than anything in the world. Her jaw jutted outward as she growled at me, "No one talks to me like that."

"She *is* a no one," Melinda sniped.

"I'll talk to you any damned way I please," I told her. "And I've got a *lot* more to say."

She raised her eyebrows and looked smug. Good. She was falling for the bait. "Oh, yeah? Maybe I've got some things to say to you, too."

"So say them."

"Do you two young ladies have something to share with the class?" I turned in my seat to find Ms. McClenny staring at me, arms crossed and mighty grim. Never mind that other kids had been talking amongst themselves while she updated her seating chart. I'm always the one who gets singled out. The whole population could be looting and pillaging while an asteroid approaches the planet, and I'd be the one arrest the police made while civilization crumbled. With my luck, it would probably be for jaywalking.

"No," I grumbled.

"No, ma'am." From around the class I heard giggles. Brian smirked at me. I wanted to wipe it from his face.

The teacher stared at us both for a moment more, like she was making some kind of point or something. Finally she ambled back up to the front of the classroom. "Get out your protractors, everyone!"

"Tomorrow. After school. Band room," I heard Brie hiss over my shoulder. Next to her, Melinda leaned forward in her seat as if crazy to know what was being said, but the message was intended solely for me. I was sure of it.

"Why not make it today?"

For a second Brie looked tempted, but her glance sidled away. "Tomorrow. And don't skip out."

"Oh, you know I wouldn't want to miss a moment of your cheddary goodness," I said back through clenched teeth.

McClenny's voice rang out loud and clear. "Victoria Marotti! Am I going to have to send you to the principal's office?"

Yeah, that's what I wanted, all right. Another trip to MacAlister's office so I could hear about how we were all the spokes on a wheel rolling to a great destination on the horizon. Whee, I say. Whee.

Addy wouldn't let me come near her after class. I spent my lunchtime eating my sack lunch behind a bush near the back of the school so I wouldn't have to see anyone. Right as I finished, it started to rain. Somehow it seemed appropriate.

I don't know. Maybe all those fake curses I'd pretended to throw had called down some kind of mad voodoo on myself. Wasn't that the way magic worked in fantasy books? Wasn't it all about balance? I didn't for a single hot second think that any of my street magic tricks brought about any actual evil-eye whammies on my classmates. Maybe, though, there was something to the idea of karma—what you dished out, you got back. Maybe it didn't matter to the karma-lized nuns or whoever handed out the points whether or not my curses were real. It could all depend on intent.

Well. I was going to have to endure a little more of the universe's backlash, then, because I was going to dish out a little more hurt into the lap of a certain Ms. Brie Layton, the blonde with a 'tude as cold and high as a three-story stack of Slurpees.

Just the thought of revenge put a certain spring in my stride. It's not like I had anything else to look forward to, right? I could deal with Addy not speaking to me. Enduring her silence and her averted glances, Tuesday and Wednesday, was tough—but I totally *got* why she was doing it. I'd be miffed, too if my best friend had ripped up my history project. Okay, I might have deserved a little misery if I'd gone all Skanky McHoHo on the only person in the world who'd devoted night and day to protecting me, but hey. Different strokes, right?

As for Dorie and Des and Ray . . . well, I made it easier for them by not hanging around. I knew them well enough. None of them wanted to get in the middle of any arguments, not even between two of their group. Keeping out of their hair solved that problem. Oh, I kept watch over them from a distance. I skulked around the school's problem spots and kept an eye on things. I hung out in the hall when lunch period let out and I made sure to swing by the hallway with Dorie's locker when she stopped off to collect her flute before orchestra. When Des emerged from her weekly Wednesday-morning meeting with the school psychologist, I was right across the hallway in the hole in the wall where the pay phone used to be, watching. I tried to keep them from seeing me so they wouldn't have to speak. But I was there for them.

One person I couldn't get out of my head, though. I kept seeing Gio's grinning face while my teachers droned on and on. Sometimes I thought about the way his smiling lips had felt against mine only a few days before. I preferred to think about him smiling. The picture of how I'd wiped away that smile didn't bear remembering. I didn't want to see him in person, that was all.

Like that was possible. Fillmore was the city's only public high school and we had hundreds of kids, but you kept bumping into the same people all day long. When I saw Gio from a distance, I'd turn down a side hall or reverse directions and scurry away. If he came out of a classroom when I walked by, I'd try to quicken my pace. I avoided the clusters of classrooms where a lot of the junior classes were held. I didn't linger at my locker or visit his.

The only way I could cope, every time I felt a tight wrenching feeling in my chest, was to tell myself it was for the best. Really, it was. Gio didn't need me dirtying his reputation. I wanted to be Tough Vick, Invincible Vick, Vick the Great and Terrible, Vick who didn't need anybody. Admitting that I was lonely, even to myself, would bring those walls tumbling down.

A brick pried loose Wednesday afternoon, though. I'd sat through my last period thinking of nothing but of how to confront Brie. I knew she'd taken those photos. Anyone else in the school would have turned me in immediately just to get the freak in trouble. Brie, though, was an outsider. She must want something from me. Part of me was curious to find out what she thought she might get. It wasn't going to be money, that was for sure. Not from me or what was left of my family.

I wasn't going to give her a chance to lord her photographic triumph over me, though. I was going to head in, overwhelm her with my mad skills, and leave her quaking in her boots. I'd done it to every other bully in this roach motel with a president's name on it. Even so, my stomach still felt icky. I hate confrontation. It's a means to an end, but I hate that it's necessary to keep people in line.

I'm not wild about the band room at the best of times, anyway. Do you know where all that dribble goes when brass players empty their spit valves? Onto the floor, that's where. The floor that never gets mopped. "That's so *wrong*," I muttered to myself as I marched upstream through the last of the students running in the direction of the front door and freedom. I'm always amazed how quickly the school manages to clear out before the final bell stops ringing. It's like people fleeing from a nuclear plant meltdown. Which isn't a bad metaphor, considering.

"What's so wrong?" Gio asked as I stopped short from colliding with him. So intent had I been on getting to the room before Brie that I hadn't seen him rounding the corner from the band room door. He stood still and looked down at me.

Crud. I couldn't meet his eyes. Some wild part of me inside wanted to know if there was anger in his gaze, but

I couldn't raise my face. If he was angry, I'd be hurt. If he looked at me with love, it would hurt all the more. What would absolutely kill me would be if his eyes were cold and held no expression at all. I didn't think I could bear that. "Nothing," I said.

For a moment there was silence between us. "What're you doing?" he finally asked.

Oh, Gio. Oh, nummy and sweet Gio. He had no idea how badly I wanted to throw myself on him and beg him to ignore all the words I'd said Monday night. I wanted him back so much. Stuffing my hands into my jeans and shrugging like he didn't matter slaughtered me. "I'm busy," I finally said. I tried to dodge around him, but he sidled over to prevent it.

He didn't say anything, though. It might have been okay if he'd taken the offensive and gunned at me, or insulted me, or even asked what the heck did I think I was doing. The way he waited for me to speak simply drove me nuts. I tried to sidestep him once more, but he blocked me. "We're not supposed to know each other when we're at school, remember?" I finally announced, wanting nothing more than to shove him out of the way. I still couldn't look him in the face.

"Maybe I don't," he said slowly. After a moment he stepped aside. "Maybe I don't know you at all."

I looked up at him then, but he was already turning away. His face appeared as I feared it might—as expressionless and frozen as one of those prehistoric statues on Easter Island, and as distant from me. *Remember those walls,* I reminded myself sternly when I felt my resistance slipping away. *You're crazy-tough, not some girl who needs a boy to make her feel good. You're not an Addy.*

A small part of crazy-tough Vick still felt sick to her stomach, though, to know that she'd pulled off a trick to make Gio vanish from her life altogether.

Brie was already in the band room, sitting on the end of a trumpet case with her arms crossed. Was the trumpet hers? I didn't know that Brie played an instrument, much less the trumpet. Girls at this school stuck to the strings or the woodwinds, usually. Still, I was startled to see her there. She hadn't sneaked around me when I was talking to Gio in the hall. *Wait a sec,* part of me thought. *Gio came out of here, didn't he?*

She stood up, sneering. "Decided to show, I see?"

I opened my arms and spread my hands. Nothing up my sleeves! "Wouldn't have missed it for the world, pretty girl." My turn to smirk. "You ready for a little trouble?"

Every girl in the world wishes she could toss her hair like Brie. "Whatever," she said with a little yawn that was merely for show. "You're not going to lay one of those lame curses on me, are you?"

"Stupid much?" I asked her. "My curses are the real shinola. Ask anyone."

"Oh, trust me, one of your little friends told me all about your curses."

"So you know the deal, then. I lay the smack down, your hair starts falling out, you get some zits, you break a nail. . . . Ooh!" I squealed, and mimicked her clutching a finger to her chest. "And your world as you know it

135

comes to a screeching halt, ricotta-for-brains."

There was no mistaking the loathing in her eyes. "You're not going to make this easy, are you?" she spat.

"What, let you blackmail me without fighting back? Girl, I've got unearthly powers backing me you wouldn't believe."

"They must *really* be slumming." The prim way she adjusted her skirt while crossing her legs made me wish I could call down a lightning bolt. Oh, for some real magic! "Okay, then. I heard you pulled quite the disappearing act a couple of weeks ago."

Oh, yeah! I thought to myself, barely able to restrain my glee. "Right here's where I did it, in fact."

"Really? What a coincidence. Bet you can't do it again."

"Bet I can."

"Fine." She stood up and reached into her big shoulder bag to withdraw an envelope. "I've got a bunch of negatives that say you can't."

"Oh, you are so on!" I could barely keep from bouncing over to the stand where the marching band banner hung. Once again I took the rope from its moorings and unhooked it. I put my hands behind my back, held one end, and gave her the other. "Go on," I said. "Start tying."

After thinking it over for a second, she fell for the cue and started to wrap the thick braided rope around my wrists and midsection. Winning those photographs back was going to be cake. Within a minute more, she had me surrounded by the length of the rope, and started to make some complicated knots with the end I'd given her. "Not too tight," I said, pretending to be nervous. Brie smirked and kept on tucking the rope into the taut circles she'd made.

"Do some more if you don't believe me," I told her. "There's a mic cord on the floor over there. Use that if you want." Like an obedient little puppy who happened to be named after a cheese, she trotted over and came back with the thin black cord. She tucked the microphone itself into one of the braided rope loops and started wrapping me again. "I think you're in for a surprise," I told her once she'd made quick work of the second layer. I was real confident I could shuck this mess without much effort; this web wasn't half as tight as any of the ropes I'd escaped from before. She wasn't even covering me with the banner. What a simp.

"Maybe I am." Brie marched me to the instrument closet. "Then again, maybe *you* are." She shoved me so hard that I nearly toppled off balance, but I was grinning at her when she shut the door. I heard the padlock fasten outside.

Both the mic cord and the band banner rope fell around my feet in a matter of seconds. Luckily the heavy rope muffed the thud of the microphone as they fell to the tile. Once atop the instrument case shelves, I slid the snare-drum box away from the trapdoor. A moment more, and I was through the ceiling and into the inky blackness of the crawl space above. I slid the case back and let the door shut.

Boy, in a few seconds Brie was going to have the shock

of her life when I appeared to collect those photographs. While I ran as quickly and lightly as I could across the catwalk in the direction of the custodian's closet across the hall, I pictured her smug little smile freezing when I sauntered into the room with some smart remark on my lips. *And the cheese stands alone, huh?* sounded pretty good to me.

Yeah. She was going to love that one, all right. Really love it, when I opened that old trapdoor, dropped down, and surprised her. Yep, when I opened that trapdoor, all right, the tables were going to turn.

The trouble, I realized as I tugged and tugged at the hatch, was that someone had locked it.

CHAPTER TEN

Has your brain ever replayed a thought over and over again without it really sinking in? When I first learned how to ride a bike and my dad let go of the handlebars, I was so happy gliding down the street that it never occurred to me to steer the darned thing. Inside my head I kept hearing, *You're going to hit that curb . . . you're going to hit that curb!* I was so giddy at the breeze in my hair and on my face that I didn't pay a bit of attention. Ten seconds later I barreled right into the curb and banged up my knees on the concrete.

That was exactly what happened on the crawl-space grating. I was so busy calculating exactly how I was going to surprise Brie that I didn't entirely comprehend why the trapdoor wouldn't open. I pulled and pulled again. Although my brain kept telling me, *It's locked . . . hey, you! It's locked!* it took a little while to sink in. When I realized with annoyance that the hatch wasn't swinging up the way it was supposed to, I gave the knob a final tug. It wasn't stuck. It wasn't jammed. Someone had twisted the latch on the other side to the locking point.

Always check your equipment before a performance. The thought came from that same sarcastic source I'd ignored a moment before. *You weren't sloppy with Gio.* Difficult though it was to admit, I hadn't been as careful as I might have been. Yes, yes, I know—I hadn't been careful at all. I'd marched into that room angry, without as much as a quick minute's worth of preparation. I should've popped across the hall to check the trapdoor on the off chance I might have to vanish.

What a buttchop I was! If I could have stood up all the way in that tight space, I might have stomped my feet in frustration. Why in the world had I let Gio distract me at a crucial moment? It was basically *his* fault I was caught up here.

Or was I really caught? There were other trapdoors around the school. Gio and I had studied the maps closely the first time we pulled a Houdini. I knew there was another access point down the hall in the telephone closet. Problem solved right there! It would take me a minute to scamper that much farther and a little bit more time to run back to the band room. I'd probably already lost a good forty seconds. I could adjust, though. Maybe instead of bursting through the band room door and confronting Brie, I'd wait outside with my arms crossed until she got bored and came out.

Yeah, actually that was a great idea! Go, me! Bent over almost double under some heating ducts, I started to sidle down the grating in the direction of my new escape route. Wouldn't Brie get the shock of her dairy-product shelf life when she got tired of lobbing her weak little Los Angeles taunts through the instrument-room door and stepped outside to see me there, leaning against the wall as if I'd been there for hours? She was absolutely going to go home with streaks in her sho—

I heard a scraping of metal behind me. Although bulbs illuminated the areas around the trapdoors, the ceiling space was really pretty dark. Ducts and pipes that snaked around the walls and into the classrooms below cast weird shadows everywhere. When a wedge of honest-to-goodness bright light sliced through the darkness back where I'd come from, I nearly had to shield my eyes against it. Someone had lifted the trapdoor in the band storage-room and looked through. Then, as quickly as it had been opened, the hatch slammed shut.

I didn't stop to think. My heart thudded as I changed directions and scrambled back. Although I banged my shinbone against the railing of the walkway, I kept myself propelling forward. It felt as if my life depended on it. I heard a clunk below my feet a moment before I reached the door. A candle would've given more illumination than the bulb above, but I found the handle without hesitation and tugged as hard as I could.

I didn't have any problem at all hearing the message my brain sent this time: *Someone's locked it.*

Then, a moment later: *You've been set up.*

Brie! Brie had planned this all along. She deliberately lured me to the band room thinking I'd be cocky and confident and ready to show her up, and what had she done? Trapped me in the ceiling. Trapped me good and tight. I'd thought it was odd yesterday that she wanted to postpone our little face-off until this afternoon; anyone else would have wanted to get it over with that same day. What I'd put down as mere cowardice, though, turned out to be sheer cunning on her part. She'd needed time to outfox me.

That little witch had gotten the better of me, but not for long. There were other trapdoors in this school. She might have shut down two or maybe even three, but she wouldn't have been so thorough as to lock them all.

But what if she had? I thrust that gutless thought from my head. Impossible.

Once more I headed across the grating to the area over the janitor's closet, and then in the direction of the telephone closet. The crawl space was more disgusting than the school rest rooms after the time the Spanish club's Midwestern version of chile rellenos made with cheese-in-a-can had sent everyone to the toilets with the runs. Parts of the railing and ducts were covered with a half-inch-high layer of powdery mold. My nose dripped like crazy. Although the catwalk was mostly a straight shot over what I thought was probably the hall, there was one point where it angled sharply around a bunch of water pipes that swooped in and barreled down. I had to drop to my knees and crawl to get under them. Black as my clothes might have been before, I was sure they were absolutely filthy after that. I got a mouthful of the grit, to boot.

Up ahead I saw weak light spilling onto the metal grid.

I almost cried with relief. I made my way forward and fell to my already banged-up knees to grab the knob so I could pull up the trapdoor.

It was locked.

I'm not really sure how I coped after that. I remember that I felt like some malevolent force had removed every bone from my body and replaced them with paper drinking straws. Oh, they were sturdy enough for the moment, but you knew it was going to be only a few minutes before they turned to utter mush. Just like my brain. And my willpower. I always thought I was one of the most controlled people I knew. I kept my secrets close. I never exposed my weaknesses. And here I was in the near dark, cramped and coughing and sneezing and dirty and losing patience and cool by the moment.

Plus I suddenly had to pee.

From the telephone closet the grating branched off into two directions, one heading to the back of the school and the gymnasium to my right, and the other leading straight ahead to the west side of the school. I chose to keep walking ahead.

Fillmore's a big, flat, one-story, sprawling expanse of a place. It takes a good five minutes to jog from the gyms at the back to the front offices. This dismal world above the ceiling was totally unlike anything below it, though. After a couple of minutes I didn't have a clue where the heck I was. All I could keep in mind was the next little lightbulb shining ahead in the darkness before me. I yanked as hard as I could at three trapdoors in a row—all locked.

This is a nightmare, I thought right before I beaned myself on a bundle of hanging cables and fell flat on my behind. I was almost worried that the commotion would make someone suspicious and that the Doormat would catch me up there and I'd be expelled without being able to explain. Let's get real, though. My fall made less noise than, let's theoretically say, a crazed goat running down tiled hallways with three thousand and twenty-five over-size wooden beads bouncing behind him. By that point I was becoming desperate. What if Brie *had* managed to latch every ceiling access door in the entire school? What was I going to do then?

While I'd been banging myself up, my brain had been doing some multitasking. *You can go through the ceiling.* Oh, yes. Simple solution. I could climb over the catwalk's rail, drop onto the suspended ceiling two feet below, and let one of the random ceiling tiles snap under my weight. Maybe if I was very, very lucky, I'd manage not to break my neck, or gouge my eye out when I landed on a pencil, or fall onto an operational circular saw in the shop, flip the switch, and earn myself the lifelong nickname of "One-Armed Vick." Oh, yeah. That was a great solution, all right. Not.

By now my bladder was starting to ache. How long had I been up there, anyway? A half hour? An hour? I scrambled to my feet and started plodding forward again, on to the next trapdoor. You know, what really galled me most was that Brie had figured out my disappearing act. How in the world . . . ?

It was with a sickening sensation in the pit of my stomach that I remembered something Brie had told me before she'd tied me up and shoved me into the closet: one of my little friends told her all about my curses. At the time I'd let it slide right by. I'd been so cocky I assumed she meant she'd been warned of my mad rep.

She was telling me something else entirely. Gio Carson had betrayed me. He'd been in that room moments before, alone with her. He didn't bother to make up an excuse for his presence when I'd caught him red-handed. When I was first getting to know Gio, I'd mentally chewed my fingernails down to nubs wondering if his kindness was a setup for later cruelty. Worse, I'd *sacrificed* my relationship with him because I wanted his safety and happiness! For long hours I'd drilled him to improve his palming and misdirection skills. Now he was telling Brie my secrets? He'd been poison all along!

I didn't want to believe that I'd wasted all that time and effort with him. I especially didn't want to believe that I'd been so *used.* It was easier to think Gio had told my secrets to my worst enemy in the world because he'd hated me for breaking up with him.

Well, guess what, buddy boy. I had a new worst enemy now, and his name rhymed with Schmo Better-Keep-Outta-My-Way-or-There's-Gonna-Be-Some-Arson. I tugged at the last of the hatches on this branch of the walkway, angry beyond belief. If those handles had been Brie's or Addy's or Gio's heads, they would've been rolling. Since they weren't, I shook my sore fingers and started retracing my steps.

I guess it boiled down to the fact that I couldn't trust

anyone but myself, in the end. I'd been stupid to team up with someone. Or make friends, for that matter. What good did friendship get me? The first student in the history of Millard Fillmore High School whose mummified skeleton would be found in the ceiling along with all the ductwork and the pipes, that's what, with I HATE BRIE written in the dust beside my body. Problem would be that by then my rival would have been long graduated and they'd think I was some kind of French cheesephobe.

Damn them. Damn them all! I kicked the iron handrail in frustration. It made a satisfying hollow noise as it shuddered from the vibrations, but my big toe suffered for the outburst. It hurt, but it was easier to cope with that kind of pain. The throbbing owie actually made me focus, and while I sat down on the grate and rubbed my toe, I heard a small, still voice in the back of my head.

You are out of control.

Someone else had said that to me recently. Whoever it was had been right, though I hated to admit it. Here I was, wasting all this energy on hate and panic and fear instead of trying to solve the problem of getting out of this awful space. I was blaming other people for my predicament when the fault really lay with me.

I'd been the person who'd heard the words *school legend* and agreed to a goatnapping. I'd been the one who lost my concentration and ripped up Addy's paper. I'd been the one who'd been careless and allowed myself to get trapped up here. I could rant and rail and kick as much as I wanted, but none of it was going to solve anything. It was all *my* fault, and the only person who was going to do anything to fix it was me.

If I wanted my life back, I had to get back in control. My first step would have to be getting out of the ceiling before my bladder exploded.

I'd given up all hope that I was ever going to escape that moldy cave and was seriously considering the option of diving out through one of the ceiling tiles and hoping that I didn't break anything more serious than my leg, when one of the trapdoors flipped up in my hand.

For a second I thought I was dreaming, or that I'd un-attached the knob. Nope—it was an honest-to-god open hatch. I peered ahead into the darkness. I'd reached the end of the grating at the school's rear. Without my really knowing it, this trapdoor had been my very last chance. Maybe someone was looking out for me after all!

I pulled it open once more and peeked through. It was noisy below, and there was a strange, familiar smell, like soap and steam and bleach and . . . dirty sweat socks?

I closed the trapdoor once more and sat down on the grating, my head in my hands. No wonder I'd been spared. This trapdoor led to the one spot in the school to which Brie either couldn't get—or didn't want—access. The gym's shower room. The boys' shower room, to be specific. Filled with naked boys showering.

It's not as if I stared, or really saw any . . . you know . . . thingies. But you see the steam, you hear the water, you listen to a bunch of adolescent boys whose vocabulary consists of the words "Dude!" and "That rocks!" shouting over the spray of the nozzles to make complex sentences like "Dude, that rocks!" and "That rocks, dude!" and you kind of assume nudity and a certain amount of shoulder acne, you know?

Could my day get any worse? Somehow I didn't think so. There was no way, absolutely *no way* I could get down out of this miserable crawl space through the boys' shower room. Nuh-uh. Nothing doing. Not in a million years!

There were quite a few wide-open mouths thirty seconds later when my feet appeared from out of nowhere, followed by the rest of me. Using a ledge where a number of the guys had flung their towels as a foothold, I hopped down. There was a slight chance that maybe one or two people had missed my entrance by that point, but to get their attention, fate had the metal hatch slam down over my head as I hit the floor.

I bet Houdini never confronted so many astounded teenage boys in his whole career, much less naked ones. "Howdy, guys," I said, brazening it out. It's pretty surprising how jocks are pretty big talkers outside the shower room, but when they're faced, without warning, with an intruder of the opposite sex, they all clutch their jewels faster than diamond vendors in an L.A. riot.

No one said a word.

"Hey, Montrose," I said to the kid standing nearest. It was hard to recognize Chad Montrose with the wet hair and the slack-jawed expression and, well, the naked thing going on, but at least he blew water from his nose and blinked when I addressed him. "Which way's the exit?"

He started to take his hand away from his googlies and point, but in the end he thought the better of it and nodded at the opposite end of the room. That trapdoor *would* have opened over the very back of the showers. Oh, well. I cracked my knuckles, straightened my spine, and walked slowly toward the door with my eyes straight ahead. I tried to make it look as if I walked through crowded boys' shower rooms all the time, which is probably not a reputation that any sane girl my age wants, but it's better than making everyone's eardrums bleed with frightened screeches. "So what, you guys are the intramural curling team? Skeet shooting?"

"Softball," said one of the boys when I passed by.

Hey, it helped the time to pass.

I'd originally intended to get the heck out as quickly as possible, but some part of me was so gleeful at my freedom that I couldn't resist turning around when I saw Arnie Peterson standing under the sprayer closest to the door. "Hey, Peterson," I called out.

His eyebrow quirked for a second before he answered. "What?"

I pointed at his feet. "What're those you're tramping around on? Size eleven? Twelve?"

Arnie looked at me like I was totally crazed. "Why?"

I shrugged and tried to seem as unimpressed as possible. "I dunno. You know what they say about guys with big feet—I guess the only true part is how they need big shoes." I let that sink in for a minute. "Later, guys." Then, with a roll of my eyes, I added just for Arnie, "See ya, shortie."

The air in the hallway felt wonderful. I hadn't noticed until that moment how hot and sticky I was. Judging by my mold-black hands and what I could see of my clothing, I was a total mess, too. I was free, though, and to breathe fresh air again felt better than anything.

The band room door was locked when I reached it. A note on a sticky note had been attached to the wall. I ripped it down and opened it. Inside were only three words:

430 Catalpa Road

The sky was getting dark by the time I finally reached Brie's address. It was one of the nicer streets in town, not far from the school, lined with tidy little expensive houses and with those trees that hang heavy with bean pods every winter. I knew the neighborhood well. It was only a hop (without the skip or the jump) away from the Carsons'. Someone was sitting on the porch of number 430, her outline barely visible in the blue of twilight. When I turned up the sidewalk, I saw a red pinpoint of light swing from between her legs up to her mouth.

It's funny. When I was under the delusion I was going to show Brie up with my Houdini act, all I could think about was how I was going to smack her down a second time with some sharp and cutting comment. Later on in the crawl space, when I was ready to kill her, along with half of the other people I knew, all I could think about were the smart remarks they deserved. Walking up to-

YOU ARE SO CURSED!

ward her house, though, I suddenly realized I didn't have anything to say.

That was probably good. I'd burned out a lot of my anger up above the school ceilings as I rammed and battered and bashed my way around. My mistake this afternoon had been barging in like a Ghostbuster ready to kick some poltergeist butt. I'd been out of control. And how many times does it take before Vick learns her lesson and gets back under control?

Apparently three or four, but no more than that, I was determined. Oh, I was a wee bit on the irked side. I won't dispute that at all. Now I was ready to be calm Vick. Cool Vick. Vick the superior who was not going to react to anything Brie had to say.

"You look like *crap* after being up there so long," were the first words out of her mouth.

"And you do it with so little effort." Calm Vick still had a little ways to go, apparently. Brie's face twitched, but instead of carping back at me she took another long drag on her cigarette. "Your parents know you smoke those death sticks?"

"Puh-lease. My mom bums them off me." She took a final suck on the nasty thing and then ground the butt underneath her heel. "So how long did you have to bang on the door to get out?"

"Puh-lease. I'm resourceful. I got an eyeful in the boys' showers on my way out. So." I thought I'd get right to the point. "How'd you know my secret?"

She laughed. Brie away from school was different from the hair-conditioner advertisement who sat in class with

151

me. This version was tougher and, I thought, a little sadder. "I'm not one of these hick-town idiots."

"You saw me that night of the last game," I suggested. "Behind the bleacher boxes, I mean." Her tentative nod admitted it was so. Grappling to keep my resentment from rising, I added, "So you followed me."

She cocked her head down at me. "Like that was so hard. I figured you were up to something, but I thought you were spying on Melinda like a big frea—" That train of thought came to an abrupt stop, and I for one wasn't disappointed it didn't pull into the station. "I wasn't even there when you took the goat, but you know, when it sounded like the end of the world out in the hallway and I looked out the door and there *you* were, I didn't need a National Honor Society pin to figure out you were up to something. Plus," she added, "one of your little friends clued me in."

I felt fire roast my heart a little more. At this rate it would be well done before dinnertime. "Gio, yeah. I know. I figured that one out."

For a second she seemed surprised—probably that I was one step ahead of her. Finally she raised her eyebrows. "Okay."

"So what do you want, then?"

"Listen," she said. "This afternoon I only wanted to talk. Just like now. You were the one who came in all ready for a fight."

She was confirming my suspicion that I could've avoided hours in the ceiling space getting black lung disease. "Listen, cheddar-face—"

"*Stop it,*" she yelled at me.

"Don't get bent out of shape. If you were being black-mailed—"

With one fluid motion she sprang up to face me. Despite the fading light, I could see how twisted and angry her face had become. "Just *stop it!*" She practically spat the words. For a second I worried I might have to fight her. "Why are you so *mean?* I can't help my name. I didn't choose it. It's not my fault my mom and dad thought it would be cute. You're always ragging me about it. *Stop it!*"

I was afraid to say anything. In fact, I was afraid to breathe. "I *hate* this place," she continued. In a mocking voice she said, " 'Oh, you'll love it, honey. You'll make friends.' Yeah, right. Whatever!"

I felt like I had to say something. "You've got friends. You've Melinda and DeMadison and that crew." Trying to console Brie felt weird. Kind of like Superman patting Lex Luthor on the back and telling him not to get so bummed out about things, what was a little kryptonite between friends, and hey, had he heard of this nifty new stuff called Rogaine? Brie, however, stabbed me with a look that made me suddenly realize that all was not hunky-dory in the land of the Hair Club for Harpies.

She suddenly sat down on the porch again and covered her face with her hands. "I want to go home. You have no idea what it's like, being the new girl."

Oh, crud. Of all the things she could have said.

Because I did know. She was talking to the girl who'd spent the entire last thirteen months creating a lie so elaborate and detailed that it made a Las Vegas stage show look like . . . well, Gio's sad little performance at the old folks' home. I sat down next to Brie on the porch, and for a moment we listened to the leaves of the bean trees rustling overhead in the dark.

I felt horribly, horribly guilty. Yeah, I should have been writing advertising copy for Kraft with all the cheese slogans I'd come up with for Brie. I thought I was only bringing the funny, but when I looked back on all the times I'd turned her the color of a boiled lobster, I could have kicked myself. She'd really taken every nasty comment to heart.

When had I stepped over the line? I thought I had gone from Vickie the stepped-on and squashed to Vick the protector of the weak, but when had I transformed into Vick the bully who picked on the new girls? When had I become the kind of person who resented her best friend for having a boyfriend and ripped up her homework, or the persecutor who taunted someone because of her name and the way she looked?

I thought I had it all figured out when I realized no one in high school looks beyond the surface of other people. I thought I was *different* from them. And here I was, being smacked in the face that not only was I the same, but I was probably worse than most.

"Hey," I finally said, breaking a silence that had been punctuated only with the whoosh of cars passing by. "I was new girl last year. I know what it's like, all right." I heard her snuffle. I don't think she was quite crying, but she sounded on the verge. "It's not that bad here, after a while. They've got cheese-on-a-stick at the mall, you know."

Through her thick breathing I heard her laugh a little. "I don't do dairy."

"Man, you are *so* from L.A.!"

She laughed again. "You're not going to believe this, but I really wasn't going to blackmail you. Well, I kind of am. Once I figured out . . . you know . . . how you do things . . ."

I don't know about other people, but when someone's made you into a guilty softy in one sentence and then brings up blackmail in the next, it's enough to make you a little defensive. "I don't have any money."

The Laytons' front porch light flicked on overhead. I was startled to see that Brie was looking at me as if a second head had popped out between my eyebrows. "Honey?" A woman's voice came through the screen door. "I need some help with my blond highlights."

"In a few minutes, Mom," said Brie, rolling her eyes at me. We looked at each other under the light of the yellow bulb, while above our heads some bugs began to batter themselves against the fixture. "She's so weird."

"What is it you want, then?" I asked, a little sad that I didn't have a mom over whom I could roll my eyes. She regarded me for a long minute. I almost felt impatient until I looked her in the eye and saw fear there. She was trying to decide if she could trust me. Brie, the person who could ruin both me and Gio with a flick of her manicured wrist, was frightened of *me*. Maybe I was nothing more than a mean old bully. "What?" I asked, more gently.

She turned her head away and looked at the ground. "I think I'm being framed for something I haven't done," she said to her feet. "You're the only one who can tell me how it's happening. You're the only other one who knows how to pull off these tricks." She met my gaze suddenly. "Help me? Please?"

I didn't need a phone booth. I didn't need a Bat Cave. Vick the protector could swing into action without a change of costume. All I needed to hear were those very words.

Chapter Eleven

The thing I hated second-most about Melinda Scott's face was that it looked so wholesome. The kind of red-cheeked, sweet-faced, curly-blond wholesome you might have seen fluttering eyelashes in a brown sugar/cinnamon oatmeal ad, or dressed in frills and lace to sing on a religious show. Those big blue eyes would never tell you a lie, oh, no; nor would those pretty little red lips ever let fly with an insult. Melinda was the pretty girl guys wanted to date and girls wanted to have as their very bestest friend. She probably put her own photos in frames that read, FUTURE PROM QUEEN.

The thing I hated foremost about Melinda Scott's face, I decided as I regarded it through the glass pane in the yearbook office door, was that all her sweetness and sugary blond goodness disguised a personality that was plain old malicious. Talk about a wolf in sheep's clothing! Melinda was more like a constipated Tyrannosaurus rex wearing a Teletubby Halloween mask.

She was a tyrant, to boot. I watched it all slantwise through the window. A pout and a flick of Melinda's index finger would send some poor little Hair Club girl scurrying across the room to fetch her a pencil. A toss of the hair, and everyone knew she wasn't happy. A trembling lip would bring them clamoring around her, concerned looks on their face. At one point, when DeMadison looked as if she were going to disagree with Melinda, Melinda waited until the others had their heads turned before reaching out and giving DeMadison a savage pinch.

There was definitely a queen-and-worker-bee thing going on among the yearbook staff, and Melinda was royalty all the way. The worker bees were loving it, though. All except Brie, who sat at the big table sorting a bunch of her photographs, trying to pretend she didn't know I was outside watching.

"I don't have any proof," she had told me that night underneath the eaves of her porch. "I think that Melinda is skimming cream from the top of the can."

"Huh?" Those farm metaphors don't do much for me.

Brie's sigh seemed to imply she had suffered long and hard from that "huh?" "Somehow or other she's stealing yearbook money. I'm pretty sure she's going to pin it on me. I'm the *new girl*, after all. The easy target. God. It's going to come down on me and I don't know how to get out of it."

"What's this have to do with me?"

"She's doing *something* so that the money's disappearing. It shakes down every Friday after school when

158

we count up the week's receipts. We get all kinds of checks and stuff for advertising, but there's some cash in the mix, and that's the stuff that goes missing." She had watched to see if I was paying attention. "The first couple of times it happened I didn't pay attention. We all kind of watched her count out the money, and then we took it to the office and got Mrs. Detweiler, the secretary, to put it into one of those deposit envelopes. She sealed it, signed off on it, and that was that."

"I don't get it," I had said. "How do you know anything was missing?"

"Because Melinda made this big point of saying it was my job to take it to the bank on Saturday mornings. At first I thought it was kind of cool, because, you know, she was giving me this job to do and I was meeting people, and I kind of felt like one of the gang. You know?" She hurried on. My face must have pretty plainly said I had no idea what it was like to be one of the gang. "Then I got to the bank and the teller opened the envelope and counted out the money and was like, 'Honey, you didn't fill out the slip right. You must've put an eight instead of a four here.' And I was like, okay, whatever. Then it happened again the week after, different teller though. But I didn't catch on until the third time, when I got the first teller again. She looked at the deposit slip, counted the money, and said, 'Oh, honey, you filled out the slip wrong again. You've only got fifty dollars in cash here and you have a hundred and fifty on the slip.' Then she stopped and gave me this *look*. I don't know, it was like she was thinking, 'Wait a minute. I've got your number.' "

"And you think Melinda's skimming the money some-how?"

"She's the only one who touches it! It's got to be her. I know that it's not going to be very long before someone finds out that account is, like, short by a few hundred dollars, and do you think anyone's going to point a finger at Melinda? Those people all think that when she sits on the crapper, it fills with perfume and violets."

"Pretty," I commented, wincing.

"You know what I mean. I want you to come watch her Friday and tell me how she's doing it. Come on, V. Please?"

I'd already made up my mind to do it, but I had another question first. "We don't have to pretend we're friends at school, do we?"

She had wrinkled her nose. "God. No."

Through the window I watched as Melinda snapped her fingers. Boy, that guy Pavlov and his dogs had noth-ing on her, because at the sound those Hair Club girls dropped down into their seats like they were playing some life-or-death game of musical chairs. The big table at the middle of the office was an absolute mess from what I could see. For a minute I thought maybe Melinda might be palming bills and perhaps concealing a few be-neath other papers, but no. From a drawer she pulled out some kind of leather-bound portfolio. Opened up and spread atop the table, it covered a lot of the rubbish. Beside it Melinda set a lockbox from which she pulled out a stack of currency and checks. She started to sort them out on the green surface. The portfolio's inside looked a little like the kind of material you see on pool or poker tables, a kind of soft green felt.

It was just like Brie had told me. Melinda counted out the checks, added them up on a calculator, then made a notation on a little slip of paper. Then she licked her fingers and riffled through the cash, toting it up on the same paper. There really was something weird about the way she made such a show of counting the money, and for a minute I couldn't quite place why. Then it struck me—the gestures looked like a stage magician's during a trick. Very clean, very showy. Every time she made a show of separating the twenty-dollar bills and counting them aloud, it was as if she were saying, *See? Nothing up my sleeve.*

Maybe Brie was right. Maybe all this display was a scam's setup. It wasn't that I doubted Brie, exactly, but I knew how possible it was for the new kid in school to get paranoid. It had also occurred to me that Brie might be covering her tail—what if she really was skimming a few bills out of the deposit envelopes and was telling me her little saga to get me to point the finger at Melinda when it all came crashing down? Brie's anger seemed too real for that possibility, though.

Notations made, Melinda neatly stacked the bills and checks into separate piles, collected the checks into her hand, and closed the portfolio with the cash still inside. The leather folder had a zipper around the edge that she pulled tight. *Very neat,* I thought.

The girls all started to rise and head in a big group for the door, so I scampered down the hall a little and pretended I was looking at a bulletin board. I didn't want them to see me at all, but if we had to meet, I'd rather seem casual than lurky and stalkerish. They whooshed by me like a pack of giggling hyenas. Their perfume mingled together like some toxic gas developed by the military for the purposes of immobilizing small villages or groups of hormonal teenage boys. I hoped that the flouncing hair brigade would pass me by, but not all the crossed fingers in the world could have prevented Melinda from halting the group to speak to me.

The leather portfolio was still tucked under her arm when she gave me one of the biggest fake smiles ever. "Hi!" I stared at her. "You know," she said in a tone that was supposed to sound confidential and sincere, but at the same time evil enough that I knew she was planning to mock me, "I think this bulletin board is only for school club announcements, and none of the clubs actually *take* losers. If you're looking for, you know, an STD clinic, you might try the board outside the counselor's office." Her little entourage tittered with their hands over their mouths.

"Gee, Melinda," I replied, imitating her sweet 'n' sour expression down to the pursed lips. "That's real nice of you, but if I ever need that clinic, I'll just ask you for the number and address. I'm sure you have them memorized."

She looked enraged. "Hah. That was so funny I forgot you're trash."

"Forgot a breath mint too, while you were at it."

Melinda tossed her curls and gestured to her crew.

They dropped their Ooh-she-did-*not*-just-say-that expressions of disgust and followed. I tried to catch Brie's eye, but she was straggling at the back of the group, clutching her books against her chest. I waited until the hyenas had rounded the corner at the front of the school before I followed. It was okay if they'd seen me once, but I really had to keep out of sight this time.

Inside the office, the girls had spread out in front of the counter in bored poses like some kind of high school police lineup gone bad. A few of them watched while Melinda showed Mrs. Detweiler the figures, but most of them either whispered to each other or looked at their nails. Brie was one of the sharp-eyed few; I thought her eyeballs might bulge out of their sockets while the secretary filled out a deposit slip and then set to stamping the checks with the school endorsement.

Finally Melinda opened the portfolio again. The bills were still tucked inside, caught in the same bundle as when she had zipped it. Melinda didn't lay a finger on the cash. Mrs. Detweiler simply scooped it up from the leather folder, tucked it into the envelope, licked the flap, and sealed it. Then she looked at Melinda over the half-glasses perched on the end of her nose and beamed.

I watched for a few seconds more as the secretary made small talk with the girls, but already I wore a smile on my face. I knew how Melinda had pulled it off. I was pretty sure, anyway—and I really had to give her credit. Although she was getting away with theft, she was pulling off a nearly perfect magic act.

Magic has a lot in common with scams, I realized. I

should know. I'd scammed people for a year. But I was different from Melinda, wasn't I?

No matter. My work was done. It was time to make my getaway before they saw me a second time.

I nearly screamed when I turned. Addy was standing right behind me, looking at me through green eyes that had been crying. Her new hair was pulled into a sloppy ponytail, like she'd fastened it back in a hurry without a mirror. My heart thudded. How long had she been there? "What?" I said at last, when she didn't say anything.

It killed me to remember that she and I were no longer friends. She started to stammer something. I could tell she was having a hard time getting it out. "I-I don't like seeing you all alone."

Oh, so it was going to be that way. "All alone? I've got plenty of friends."

She was still trying to force out whatever she wanted to tell me. "Gio told me . . ."

My impatience flashed into anger. "You don't have any business talking to Gio." The notion of them comparing notes about me behind my back made me crazy. I didn't need them pitying me, all superior and smug. I'd do fine without their interference, thank you very much. "You've got *Bart*, don't you?" She bit her lip. "Don't you?"

I thought she might burst into tears. "No," she said at last. "I don't."

Oh, I knew it! This was rich. For a moment I managed to forget why I was in the school's front hallway to begin with. "So now Bart's dumped you and you want to come back and be my friend again? I always told you he was a buttchop, but man, did he ever pull the wool over your eyes." She at least had the decency to flush and look embarrassed at my accusations. I knew I was on the right track. "He got you to change; then he dropped you. I figured you'd run back to me, all boo-hooing your eyes out, when you saw his true colors." There. Let her deal with a dose of truth.

Her voice was low when she dropped her face to the tiles below our feet and spoke. "He was a buttchop. You were right. But he didn't dump me . . . I dumped him." She must have seen the surprise on my face when she looked up. "It's true. He didn't want me to go. But I'd realized—*ew*. Bart *Nelson*. If he'd been worth having as a boyfriend I wouldn't have kept it a secret for so long, right? I think I was with him because . . . I wanted to see if I could."

I didn't know what to say to that. I hadn't expected it at all. "Wow." Behind me I heard the latch to the school office clack open, followed by the sound of voices.

Creeeezus. The Hair Club was going to catch me again. If they saw this little conspiratorial clinch, they'd know I was up to something for sure. Addy was still talking. "I swear to God, Vick, I didn't change for him. I did it because I wanted to. For *me*. Then when you started to spend so much time away from me . . . I didn't realize that you and Gio—"

"I don't know," I said helplessly. Behind me I heard footsteps from the office into the corridor. It was too late to run, but a plausible reason for hanging around might

165

distract their suspicions. I might have been detained further. I clutched Addy's arm and interrupted her. "I can't explain," I said in a whisper, "but I really need you to pretend to be very, very angry with me right now. Just—"

Before I'd finished my thought, Addy slapped me. Slapped me? Holy cats, she hauled off and socked the right side of my face so hard that I reeled back and banged against the wall. The babble behind me turned to shocked silence as Addy advanced on me. "You don't *listen* to me!" she screeched.

For a second I was frightened she might backhand me again. I mean, I wanted her to act convincing, but holy cow, I had no idea she had an Oscar-destined career skulking around inside her. "You *boss* and *boss* us around but you never listen to a thing we tell you! Forget it. Just *forget it!* I haven't liked you in a long time!" Her face was close to mine and her fingers gripped my forearm so tightly I worried she was cutting off circulation. "You know," she finally said in a voice so level and calm that it sounded as if it were coming from someone alien, "I don't care if I ever see you again." She released my arm with a shove so violent that I banged into the wall again. "Bye-bye . . . *freak.*"

With a look of utter loathing in my direction, Addy turned and walked away. I was absolutely stunned. She had been acting, right? Then why did it feel so . . . real? And final? If I'd scripted the scene myself, I would have thought her final words a masterpiece send-off. So why did it hurt so much to hear them coming from her mouth?

"I'd say the Kornwolf is showing good taste in more ways than one, these days," Melinda commented as she flounced by. "Later, witch."

To be totally honest, it didn't totally surprise me when Melinda shaped two of her fingers into the letter L, held them against her forehead, and mouthed the word *loser* before she sauntered down the hall with the Hair Club. I mean, that L-thing is *so* three years ago.

That's okay, though. My reply only needed one finger.

I had to inspect my face in the mirror when I got home. My cheekbone was a little red, but the blow left no serious damage. My head spun not so much from the punch as from Addy's apology. My poor brain was overwhelmed with information. Addy had broken up with Bart? That was a plus in her favor. She wanted to be friends again? Fine. I could deal with that, eventually. But when had she talked to Gio? And why? What in the world had they said?

There was only one way to find out. I went into the kitchen and dialed Addy's number. Yes, dialed. Our tiny kitchen had the house's only phone, an ancient rotary model built into the wall.

After six rings, I hung up.

Okay, so where was she, if she wasn't with Bart? It wasn't like she had a life outside either him or me. No, that was mean. I felt ashamed for thinking it. Of course she had a life. I hated the notion that sometimes it didn't include me. For a week I'd been mad at her for lying and running around behind my back. To be completely honest, I would've been equally as angry if she'd told me the truth. I'd neglected her for Gio and lied about it. I couldn't afford to be self-righteous.

Gio. I could call Gio and ask him what they'd talked about.

I'd already let my finger spin around the dial seven times and heard half a ring when suddenly I came to my senses and slammed the receiver down. Gio wouldn't want to talk to me. What had I been thinking?

I'd barely taken my hand away when the phone started to ring. I froze. Did Gio know I'd called? Did Addy? It took a lot of willpower to lift the receiver out of its metal cradle and growl out a hello.

"Hey, V. Did Addy kick your butt or *what?*" Brie laughed like it was the first time she'd been able to draw a breath all afternoon. Given the way I'd seen Melinda ordering the girls around, it wouldn't surprise me if that was the case. "I was like, *dude!*"

"She was faking." It took a lot of restraint on my part not to call Brie a cheese name at that point, but I managed.

"Is that your answer? Survey says . . . she and Melinda were pretty palsy-walsy after you left."

I froze at the words. It couldn't be true. Addy could never be palsy-wa . . . I mean, *pals* with Melinda Scott. She had faked the hatred behind that punch. Hadn't she? "What do you mean?"

"Not a big deal. Just Melinda telling her they were going to be real good friends from now on. The same kind of stuff she used on me. You'd better face it, V. Red's gone over to the dark side. So, did you figure out Melinda's deal? I'm not going crazy, right?"

"You're not." I was. Slowly and surely I was going crazy. I didn't understand anything now. Had Addy really freaked out on me? Maybe she thought I wasn't taking her seriously. I felt feverish and miserable at the thought that I might have messed up my one shot at getting Addy's friendship back.

Brie stood my silence as long as she could. "V? So did you figure it out?"

"Oh. Yeah, yeah, I did. Listen. Can I call tomorrow and give you the details?"

"Sure thing. Oh, man, I can already tell I'm going to sleep better tonight. So how are we going to turn her in? Do we call the cops? Get the veep on board?" When I didn't answer, she explained, "You know? Your friend Dermot?"

"I think I should talk to her alone." It was difficult to talk and think at the same time. I rubbed my still-sore cheekbone. "Can you figure out when I can get her alone Monday? I want to keep you out of it as much as possible . . . less trouble for you in the end."

"I'll figure it out." I was about to cut the call short when, after a brief silence, she said, "Hey, Vick. You're not too bad, you know."

"Listen," I said, feeling sadder than I could ever explain in words. "You're going to give me those photos, right? Monday? I don't have to worry about them?"

"Sure thing." Her tone was bright and cheerful. "No

hard feelings, right? I never liked that stupid statue of President Whoever, anyway."

"No hard feelings," I promised as I hung up the phone.

I felt as if I'd traded relief for grief, and come up short in the bargain. I could breathe easy again knowing those photos no longer threatened either me or Gio, but now I had to live with the possibility that I'd lost my best friend for the second time in a week. It hurt like hell the first time. This round was shaping up to be worse.

I called Addy's house again. No answer.

Maybe I wasn't the sort of person made to have friends. I could be one of those perpetual loners doomed to wish she could be on the inside for once, instead of the outside. I'd almost had an inside here. Maybe the losers' club weren't the most popular kids, or the prettiest, or even the most normal, but they really had been my friends. I missed going shopping for boys' clothes with Ray, or watching television with Dorie and Des and Addy. I missed having someone to talk with over lunch.

I missed Gio.

Look how I'd messed up. I'd twice pushed away my best friend and avoided the others for fear of what they might say. I'd thought awful thoughts about all of them—hatred at Addy for lying to me, anger at the others for siding with her, and terrible, murderous thoughts against Gio for ratting me out to Brie. I'd badmouthed them to their faces and lied. At that moment I desperately wanted them all back.

It was kind of funny, really. I'd built up this tough witch-chick exterior so people would stay away. Now that

I was totally and utterly alone, I didn't want to be by myself.

Maybe I *was* the sort of person who could have friends. Maybe I was the sort of person who hadn't treated mine well. But that could change, right?

I could fix things. Right?

By the time I finished dialing the last number, my hands shook with fear. This call was one of the most difficult things I'd ever done. *One ring.* I'd wait until five before I hung up. *Two rings.* Five would be acceptable. Most people answered by five rings. *Three rings.*

"Hello?"

I hadn't expected him to answer, and any courage I'd screwed up when I'd spun out his number had vanished. The warmth of Gio's voice took my breath away. No, I mean literally. I was so frightened at the sound that I was gagging and trying to suck in a lungful of oxygen before I suffocated and passed out. "Hello?" he said again.

How did I get myself into these messes with him? I thought I might salvage the situation by speaking up, but every time I opened my lips, I couldn't find the words. A few more seconds passed without either of us saying anything. Why didn't he hang up? Why didn't I? If I said anything now, I'd seem like a total doof.

"Vick?" If a heart attack feels like someone had stood me in a wading pool and then held a live electrical wire against my chest, that's pretty much what I had at the sound of my own name. And still I couldn't reply. "I know it's you," he said. "We have caller ID."

"Oh. Hi," I managed to breathe out. I tried to sound casual. "How's it going?"

There was a curious pause at the other end of the line. "You're not getting, like, all stalkery on me, are you?" he asked. "You know, following me around school, leaving obscene notes in my lunch bag? I'm not going to come home and find my pet bunny boiling on the stove?"

He wasn't slamming the phone down yet. He wasn't cold and silent. Joking at least gave me something I could work with. "Once you've finished getting over yourself, I wanted to ask you a couple of questions."

"Come on over, then," he told me.

That stopped me dead in my tracks. Talking to Gio now, after everything that had passed between us, was difficult enough. I couldn't see him in person. Certainly not in his neat, orderly house, surrounded by everything that reminded me of what I'd never have and what I'd never be. My time with Gio had been the closest I'd ever come to that kind of life. "I can't," I told him.

This was the thing: I didn't want Gio back. Oh, on some level I wished I hadn't been forced to leave him. Yet hadn't I accused Addy of running back to a friendship she'd abandoned? To suggest such a thing to Gio would cheapen my feelings for him. I couldn't tell him I'd changed my mind now that Brie was no longer a danger. Gio wasn't a disposable razor I could fish out of the trash for one more go at the old leg stubble. "I'll come over there, then," he said. When I started to protest, he broke in. "Don't bother saying no. I've got stuff I want to say to you, too."

"You can't come here," I said weakly. I looked around the kitchen with its chipped stove and sad, peeling wallpaper and its microwave oven that probably had been in use since the Civil War.

"Guess what? I'm gonna. Give me your address. Vick." His voice was insistent. "I've never seen where you live. Give me your address."

I whispered it to him and hung up the phone. This city wasn't that big. He would be here in less than ten minutes. What could I do to pretty up the place in six hundred seconds so that it didn't seem so . . . dire?

Nothing. I'd spent so much time in the last year trying to appear to be anything but what I truly was. Let him see the real me, in my real home. Let Gio see me without my layers and layers of protection, without my attitude. Let him see me naked.

Er, no. Not *naked* naked. I don't know where that one came from. But allowing him in my home would let him see exactly why I wasn't any good for him. So I didn't clean up my dad's piles of magazines from around his favorite chair, and I didn't put away the collection of soda-pop cans accumulating on the kitchen counters so we could return them for cash. I didn't hide away the afghan my mother had crocheted before I was born, despite its holes you could pass a basketball through. I sat on the sofa and waited, flinching every time I heard a car drive down the street.

It wasn't long until I heard the grinding of tires, the silence of an engine shutting off, and the double chirp of a car remote triggering the alarm. Gio's keys jingled as he approached the porch. When he pounded on the battered screen door, my heart seemed to echo the rhythm. I admitted him without a word, and sat down before my legs could give way

"Hi," Gio said at last, staring at me. When I wouldn't meet his gaze, his head turned. I gave him time to take in the living room. Every passing moment made me more and more uncomfortable. When he looked at the love seat with the arms clawed and battered by the previous tenant's cats, it felt like someone had flicked the tongue of a whip across my back. It stung when he glanced at the dirty coffee mug with the broken handle by my dad's favorite chair, or looked at the carpet with its old pet-pee stains. I felt another nip when he looked at the cardboard covering a broken windowpane the landlord still hadn't fixed. I expected him to sneer when he spotted the vase of hideous felt flowers on the table next to me. Then he looked once more in my direction.

He knew now. He knew what kind of person I really was, and why I was bad for him. I wasn't from his little world of greeny furniture sets and college catalogs on the coffee table. This rented house was where I lived. This was a part of me I wanted people never to see. I waited for him to make an excuse to leave, or look at his watch and begin, "I don't have much time. . . ." That's the kind of treatment he should be giving me.

Instead he finally sat down in my dad's chair and crossed his arms. "You know," he said, "I really want to like you, but you don't make it easy."

Ow. That stung, but I couldn't deny the charge. I bit

my lip and collected my thoughts, willing my tears to stop puddling. "I want to like you, too.".

"Do you?"

He looked so defensive. It was with a shock that I realized we were almost mirror images, the way we sat across from each other with crossed arms and hurt expressions. It made me feel protective of him, but I resisted the urge to tell him the things I didn't want to say. "Gio, don't. All I wanted to ask was why you and Addy talked this week."

He seemed surprised. "Addy? What's she got to do with anything?" It was as if he'd told me he had three weeks to live and I'd said that was all very nice, but did he know the channel number for MTV? He shook his head, baffled, and stammered, "She told me she was worried about you. She asked if I thought you were okay." I waited for him to go on. "I told her I didn't know. I didn't know you'd let her in on . . . you know."

"I didn't. Not much." Part of me was relieved to know Addy had genuinely cared enough to take a chance and call him. The rest of me wished that Gio were far away in his nice little neighborhood and that I could be alone. On the sofa. Hiding under my mother's afghan. For the entire summer.

"She was worried you were going to get into a fight, and kind of asked me to check it out. That's all. Was I not supposed to talk to her?"

I thought hard. If Addy had overheard something about Brie and me meeting, and had said something to Gio so that he stopped by the band room that afternoon . . . But why would Addy feel any responsibility at all toward me after what I'd done to her? It was utterly . . .

"Oh, oh, oh!" I exclaimed, sitting up. Suddenly I saw it all. "You didn't tell Brie I wasn't a witch, did you!"

He wrinkled his forehead. "Jeez, no! When I looked in, she was sitting there alone. I don't think she knew who I was. When I ran into you, you were in such a mood I figured you could handle her fine." He blushed. "To be honest, I almost thought you deserved it. But I didn't want you ganged up on. Why would I tell anyone you weren't a witch?"

"You didn't. Addy did." It made total sense. While she was seeing Bart, Addy had spilled the beans to Brie that I was using street magic. Accidentally, perhaps. Maybe to get back at me. No wonder Brie had acted weird when I'd suggested that Gio was her informant! When Brie seemed to be after me, Addy felt guilty and turned to Gio for help. What did she think would happen? Band room Jell-O catfighting?

Wait a hot minute. Since when did Addy know that I wasn't a witch?

"Did you think I'd told Brie Layton our secrets?" I liked the way he said her name with a little bit of incredulity. "Is that why you . . . stopped what we had?"

"No," I was able to say quite truthfully. This was my chance to be honest, my opportunity to make amends. That's what I wanted, right? "Gio, listen. I'm not what you want. I'm not pretty. I'm not in the top percentile on my test scores. And look at this place!" I waved my hands around at the shabby living room.

He followed my instructions and looked at it again. "What's wrong with this place?"

"I know you think it's a pit!"

He shrugged. "Seems comfortable to me." Gio leaned forward on the edge of his chair until he was only a few inches away. "I think you're very pretty," he said, brushing my hair away from my forehead.

No, he shouldn't be touching me. I wanted to draw back . . . but oh, I couldn't. "I'm a deadbeat."

He turned his right hand so that I could see it, front and back. "Could a deadbeat teach me how to do this?" I felt his fingers brush the edge of my ear as he reached behind it. With a smooth motion, he plucked a quarter from the air and turned it so that it glittered in the lamplight. Or not really. The quarter was covered by lint and some sticky goo, and I suspected he'd found it in the recesses of my dad's chair. But had it been gleaming and fresh from the mint, it couldn't have been more beautiful.

Gio had been practicing. The clumsy boy I'd first known could never have pulled that off. "That's all very nice, but—"

He reached behind my other ear and produced a stick of spearmint gum. When he pressed it into my hand with the quarter, it was already warm and pliable.

"Gio—"

A rubber band snapped out of my nose, and then he managed to find a pencil stub in my hair. With every new place he found an object, I felt the gentle warmth of his skin close to mine.

I couldn't help but laugh when he made a show of

wrenching a pocket comb from his own nostrils. He sniffed long and deep when it came out, shook his head, widened his eyes, and grinned at me. "I don't know where I'll be after next year, Vick. I could be at a college halfway around the world. But that's a long time in the future, and I like you now." He started to cough right then. I thought he'd choked on his own spit or something, but a second later he was bent over and was racking his lungs to expel . . . oh. He held out his hand to produce his car key and remote.

"*That* was sanitary," I said wryly. Did Gio know how easily he charmed the socks off of me? It was true. I'd be absolutely sockless at that moment if I weren't already barefoot. The corners of my mouth trembled while I struggled to conceal the smile bubbling up from within. "Pockets empty? Are you done yet?"

He twined his fingers together and cracked them, then wiggled them in one of the casual moves I'd taught him. While he stared at me intently, he pointed one set of fingers at my eyes, as if pretending to hypnotize me. When he reached out and stroked my hair, I could feel that he'd left something behind. I reached up and plucked out one of the dingy, dirty felt flowers that had been sitting in the vase on the side table. As I stared at it, its long wire lying across my palm, all I could say was, "Oh, Gio."

"Let me make my own choice about whether you're good enough for me," he whispered. "You've been very good for me so far."

My voice sounded shaky as I heard myself rasp out,

"No more big stunts, though. No school legends. No secrecy."

"No secrecy. Those kids are a rotten audience anyway. If we play that goat-disappearing act at Shady Pines, though, they'll be peeing their Depends." I laughed. There was nothing else I could do. "Can you trust me?" he asked.

I had decided on my answer long before he asked. Of course I would trust him. How could I not? While he watched, I separated my hands from the flower they enclosed. Its stem wobbled for a moment as my hands drew farther apart and out in his direction. Together we watched it with mingled gazes, our smiles meeting in that space between us where the flower floated in midair.

CHAPTER TWELVE

"You know what your problem is, Marotti?"

It was a question I seemed to get a lot. I leaned over the yearbook table, looked Melinda Scott square in the eye, and cut her off. "As a matter of fact, I do. My problem is that I dislike bullies taking advantage of the weak. My *problem* is that bullies like you pick on your victims because of the way they dress, or the way the look, or how much they weigh, or even because of the people they love, and that when you do it, you think you have the right. That's my problem."

I could have been giving the Gettysburg Address in Swedish for the impact it had. Throughout my speech she rolled her eyes and blinked her eyelashes so rapidly that she threatened to stir up a sirocco. The entire time her mouth was pursed into a perfect little point. Suddenly I felt very sorry for her mother. "Are you done?" she finally said.

"Girl, I'm just getting started here." When her eyes

flicked over my shoulder, I turned my head and saw several permed heads jockeying for position to look through the glass pane in the door. "Don't worry. We don't need your friends to hear about this."

"If you touch me—"

"Oh, I'm not going to lay a hand on you."

"What are you going to do, curse me?" She spat the word *curse* as if it tasted bitter on her tongue.

I held up my hands. "My cursing days are over." Well, the school had seen the last of my witchy curses, anyway. I still enjoyed a good swear word now and then.

"Whatever. I'm opening the door."

I sidestepped in front of her before she could walk across the room and release the lock. "I thought I'd spare you the drama of having your friends hear about the three hundred and fifteen dollars you've stolen."

That stopped her, all right. She stared at me with fear in her eyes. The moment passed; her eyelids drooped to conceal her gaze. "I don't know what you're talking about."

"Okay. Whatever. Maybe I'll fetch Vice Principal Dermot and tell him what I saw."

She leaned against the side of the big table and took small glances at me to see if I was bluffing. "I don't know what you think you saw, but you couldn't have seen me steal money. What did I do, stuff it down my bra? If there's money missing, one of the other girls must have taken it. I can check the books. . . ."

A good magician can spot misdirection when she sees it. Melinda was trying to lead me astray. "That was the best part of your little scam, wasn't it? Their eyes watched you walk off with the money, but their brains didn't realize what was going on."

Her perfume suited her, I decided. I got a whiff of the stuff as she tried once again to push by me. It was sweet as a rose, but sharper than its thorns. "I don't have to listen to this."

"Let's say I had a big book, but between its covers was only one page," I told her. "Let's say I'd bound it in leather. Maybe the inside covers and the page were made out of the same material—like, for example, green felt." That got her attention. She sat back down again and stared at me with deadly loathing. "Maybe it's not a book. Maybe it's a portfolio with a zipper, and when it's open, that one leaf in the center tucks nicely into the side, so that no one knows there's more to it than meets the eye. All they see is a perfect surface for counting money on top of a messy desk."

"I have better things to do than sit around here all day and listen to this stupidity," she said.

"Stupidity? Nah. It's a clever trick, Melinda. Every week before your Friday meeting you would tuck some of your own cash into one half of your little folder—a thick stack of fives and tens. Sixty dollars one week, fifty the next, maybe. That would be the half your little posse wouldn't see when you opened up the portfolio on the table." I rapped the wood with my knuckles. "All they saw was a blank surface. Why would they think there was more? Then you'd count out that week's receipts—maybe a hundred dollars one week, a hundred and twenty the next."

Melinda looked positively white. As for me, I felt calm and serene and at peace with the world—not! My heart pounded so fast that I felt like I'd run a marathon, but this felt *good*. Briefly I wondered if those detectives on television felt this way when they nailed a perp, because if so, I was changing my career track to law enforcement, and fast. I was loving this. From behind me I heard a tapping at the window. Melinda looked up, shook her head, and shooed away the person trying to get her attention. She wore a terrible expression. It was the face of an evil stepsister realizing the glass Doc Martens fit Cinderella perfectly.

"So here's how it worked. Right here on this table, in front of all those girls, you'd zip up the portfolio with a hundred and twenty of the school's bucks in one side, and sixty of your own in the other. Then you'd all trot along to the office and present the cash to Mrs. Detweiler. Only when you'd unzip the folder, you made sure the side that opened was the side with the smaller amount of cash, didn't you? But you were careful to keep out the checks. If you'd opened up the portfolio and they'd disappeared, that would look awfully funny. Mrs. D. never counted the cash. Why should she, when all the other girls had watched you total it twice? She'd write out a deposit slip for one hundred and twenty dollars, but seal only half that in the envelope. Then you could walk out of the building with a cool sixty-dollar profit tucked under your arm. Week by week you did it, to a grand tune of three hundred and fifteen dollars."

"Brie," Melinda said in a growl. "Brie's behind this."

"*You* were behind this," I corrected her, taking a breath to damp down the glee I felt. "Brie was the one you picked to take the fall. The new girl. It's easy to pick on the new girl, isn't it? But she was pretty enough and dressed well enough that you could pretend she was your friend. For a while, at least, until someone noticed money missing. Then you planned to point a finger at her. You made it look like she was dipping into the deposit envelope—but the trick of it was that the money was gone before the envelope was sealed." I let it sink in for a second. "You're my problem, Melinda. People like you have always been my problem."

Out in the hallway the bell rang. Lunch was over. Through the closed door I could hear the babble of voices and of lockers opening and shutting rising to overwhelm the silence between us. "What are you going to do?" she said at last. "Tell Dermot and MacAlister?"

"Not if I don't have to," I told her. We didn't have much time left. I had to be in history class in five minutes. "Want to hear the deal?" She nodded, biting her lip. "At two-thirty this afternoon we're meeting after school. You're going to bring three hundred and fifteen dollars. While I watch, you're going to take it to the office and have a deposit slip made up for it. I don't care if you have to skip class to go home and get the money. I don't care what excuse you have to make up to get the books straight—that's your concern. I'm here to see you make things right. Any questions?" She shook her head.

"Good. Two-thirty." I picked up my backpack and without a word of good-bye, made for the door.

"You can tell Brie she's relieved of all yearbook duties," Melinda snapped as I opened the door. "I don't want to see her ugly face again."

I glanced back over my shoulder. "Sorry to get all Forrest Gump on you, Melinda, but pretty is as pretty does, and girlfriend, at this point even Revlon couldn't give you enough of a makeover."

The Hair Club scattered when I unlocked and jerked open the door. For a moment they looked as if they were going to rush in and console their queen bee for having to endure the torture of my presence for ten whole minutes, but when Melinda slammed the door shut behind me, I guess they got the message that she wanted to be alone. I saw a familiar face among the haze of hair spray. "Addy!"

But it was too late. Her copper hair whipped around as she turned her back to me. A moment later Addy was walking down the hallway and whispering something into DeMadison Cook's ear. I'd come out of the yearbook office feeling alive—vibrating, really, with righteous energy. One parting glance and a toss of red hair was all it took to drain my vitality.

"Hey." Gio pushed himself away from the wall where he had been leaning a little farther up the hallway. He had a pack full of books slung over his shoulder. His presence didn't erase the sadness I felt at losing Addy, but it still made me smile to see him. "Give her time," he said.

185

"She'll come back around again. She really was worried about you last week."

"I don't think so," I told him. "I think it's for good this time." Saying the words aloud felt awful, but I didn't see any other explanation for Addy's behavior. I'd ruined our friendship for good.

He gazed off after the gaggle of Hair Club girls in the distance. "It's not much, but can we maybe walk to class together?"

Of course! I could walk with him in public now. I was surprised at how good it felt to anticipate such a simple pleasure. "Yeah." I grinned at him as we hooked our thumbs into our shoulder straps and started to push through the noisy crowd. The warning bell clanged loudly about our heads. "I'd really like that."

I managed to catch Brie between history and biology. I guess she took the news pretty well that Melinda wanted nothing more to do with her. I mean, if you call it a positive reaction when someone falls down onto her knees and shouts "Hallelujah!" at the top her voice so that everyone in the hallway grows deadly silent and then giggles and goes about their business. "You *so* rock!" she said, jumping up and hugging me around the neck. Then she brushed off her sweater and her pretty floral skirt and smoothed down her hair.

"Happy, I take it?"

"I want to be there with you this afternoon," she told me. "I know, I know what you're going to say. I shouldn't be involved. She already knows, though, V. I'm home free at this point. Oh." She began digging into her over-the-shoulder book bag. "Speaking of home free."

Brie handed me a plain manila envelope. Merely by running my fingertips across it I could tell it was the incriminating photographs she owed me. Funny thing: I really didn't think she'd stiff me on the photos after I'd helped her, but it surely felt good to have them in my hands at long last. They were getting shredded the minute I got home. "Thanks."

"The negatives and everything are in there, too. You know . . ." She shifted from foot to foot, looking uncomfortable. Kids kept streaming by us in both directions. "I'm glad things turned out the way they did. Thanks."

Okay. So maybe Brie and I were going to have to renegotiate that not-pretending-to-be-friends clause, because right at that moment I knew I'd never call her dairy-based names ever again. Or maybe, just maybe, we perhaps weren't pretending. Not much, anyway.

I didn't think I'd ever get through biology and Spanish that day. I mean, I didn't give a rip where the house of Pepe was, or who was the prettiest señorita in the pueblo. All I could do was watch that clock on the wall and try not to squirm. Swear to God, it felt like there was a party in my stomach and all my internal organs got invited, only the kidneys got into a catfight and my spleen got busted for a fake ID, while all the rest did the limbo.

The bell finally rang at two-fifteen. I sighed and put away my Spanish book before giving Señorita Wiggins a hearty *adios*.

Gio waited for me outside. "You ready?" he asked.

My lips formed a small hole as I exhaled. I could picture

how that sigh would look if I'd done it outside in cold weather: a perfect column of white air. Finally I nodded. "Let's go."

Although Melinda had agreed to my terms during our lunchtime confrontation, I still worried that somehow she would try to weasel her slimy little way out of it. I'd only given her a couple of hours' head start for two reasons. First, I knew she could get her hands on that amount of cash pretty easily at home, and quickly. Second, I didn't want to give her time to think up some scheme to get back at me. Hell's bells, if I was in her place, I'd be trying to mastermind some devious little plot, too.

In two hours, though, I didn't think she'd be able to grapple with more than the two options I'd given her. Either she could cough up the money and some lame excuse why it hadn't been deposited with the rest, or she could deal with ol' Doormat after I had a little talk with him, *mano a witcho*.

Gio and I were approaching the yearbook office when Ray came strolling down the hall from the opposite direction. He stopped in front of us, arms crossed, glowering. Desiree and Dorie were right behind him. I almost felt like I was being ganged up on. For over a week I'd been watching over these three from around corners, but I hadn't seen them all together since . . . well, for a long time. Was I supposed to act casual? Did they expect me to apologize?

"I got a bone to pick with you," said Ray in his gruff tenor.

"Listen, guys," I said, meeting all their eyes. "I know

I've been a bad friend lately, but can this wait a few? Honest, I've got to—"

"No, it can't," Dorie piped up. It surprised me, as she's usually the quietest of the three of them.

Ray and Gio exchanged nods. I thought it was a bit odd, until I remembered they were in the same English class. "We've got a couple of minutes," Gio told me. "Relax and hear what they have to say."

He started to help me remove my backpack. I felt more secure with it on, as if I could zoom away without warning. I let him ease it down from my shoulder, though, and onto the floor behind me. Gio rose, then faced my three friends with me. I appreciated his support.

"You've been totally on the sly of late," Ray said. What was that smudge under his lower lip? A soul patch, apparently. I had a confused moment in which I remembered that, biologically, Ray wasn't the right sex to grow thick facial hair, but then I realized he'd penciled it in with eyeliner. Clever.

"You don't like us anymore." Dorie looked from Gio to me.

"Guys, listen," I began.

From behind me I heard some rustling noises and the sound of a zipper being undone. I started to turn, but Gio placed his hand on my shoulder. I figured it was some kid at his locker. "Vick's been busy," Gio said.

Ray wore a look of annoyance. His lip curled. "Yo, yo, what's this *busy!* You too *busy* to hang out with your *friends?*"

"Why don't you come to lunch anymore?" Desiree

189

asked. "I haven't bitten my nails for three days."

"And I haven't had dessert all week," Dorie added.

I had missed it all. I felt horribly guilty. To be confronted this way was awful, but I knew I deserved it. "Guys, I'm really sorry," I said. "I swear. Give me ten minutes, and then we can all sit down and—"

Once again I heard the zipping sound behind me. "What's going on?" I heard Brie ask, her footsteps approaching from behind. Gio's grip tightened on my shoulder blades when he felt me try to turn once more. Instantly I grew suspicious.

A good magician can spot misdirection when she sees it, remember? I was being distracted, deliberately, by my three friends. What was more, Gio was in on it; he was actively trying to keep me from looking around. This was not good. I whirled in my spot.

My heart nearly stopped to see Addy Kornwolf behind me. Her hair was still swaying from her having just risen to an upright position. Farther back, Brie was staring from Addy to me, puzzlement written all over her face. I was right there with her.

What in the world had Addy been up to? Absently I clutched at the seat of my pants, wondering if she'd been attaching a KICK ME sign there. Maybe that was too juvenile? Then why had she been down on the floor?

"What the f . . ." My curse trailed off as I realized exactly what she'd been doing. My backpack. The one sitting on the floor. The backpack that Gio had helped remove from my shoulders—she'd been rummaging inside it.

Right at that moment, Vice Principal Dermot rounded the corner. His heels made a rapid tapping sound on the tile like gunshots. Behind him trotted Melinda and the rest of her entourage. *Curses!*

"You!" His cry echoed along the hall. "Marotti. Don't you *dare* move!"

All my old suspicions flared. I stared wildly around at the five of my so-called friends. I'd been set up. I'd been royally had. While the heat flamed my face, I staggered back against the wall. My so-called friends were against me after all. Every single one of them! I didn't have a person in the world I could trust.

It felt like falling off the top of a skyscraper with no net to catch me. With every step that drew Dermot closer, I accelerated and plummeted toward my doom.

"—and when I looked up, the envelope was gone!" Melinda was complaining. "It had to be her! She took three hundred and fifteen yearbook dollars! The hard work and labor of the yearbook staff! I saw her putting it in her backpack!" I froze. My backpack! Addy had put the money in it!

"Yes, yes, Ms. Scott, I heard you the first time. Marotti!" Gio and the others scattered to the side as the vice principal strode up to me. Traitors, every one of them. I couldn't meet their eyes. "I think it's my lucky day—the day I get to expel you. Got anything to say about that?"

I leaned against the wall, unable to speak. Tears began to blur my eyes. "Please," I said. I'd never anticipated this turnaround. Melinda had made Addy her stooge and then fabricated a twisted version of the story for the

191

Doormat to throw all the blame on me. I'd been outwitted. Thoroughly skunked. For me school was out—forever.

"It's too late for *please,* missy. You've gone way too far this time." He knelt down on the floor and grabbed my backpack so he could wrench open the zipper. "A manila envelope, you say?"

Melinda paused her crocodile tears long enough to comment in her normal nasty voice, "An eight-by-eleven sealed manila envelope." While the Hair Club girls cast ugly looks my way and consoled their leader, the vice principal hauled out my massive biology textbook and tossed it on the floor. The sound echoed like a cannonball.

I still felt as if I were taking a nosedive. My body felt heavy and weighted down. I blinked to clear my eyes, but only saw Addy staring my way. Addy, my former best friend. Addy, who had utterly betrayed me. I never thought she'd hate me as much as she did.

Then she winked at me. I almost didn't catch it. The corners of her lips trembled slightly, as if she were trying not to smile. But she had winked at me! Addy caught Gio's eye and then looked back at the Doormat.

A sudden surge of hope made me catch my breath. When I looked at Gio, he only met my glance briefly. He, too, had a tiny smile playing on his lips. Dorie looked at the floor. Desiree gnawed at her lip, but her eyes sparkled a little. And Ray! Ray was outright smirking! It was as if they all shared a joke with each other—as if they had played a prank, but not against me. I was somehow part of their circle.

"I'll find it," growled the Doormat. The pile of notebooks and texts on the floor grew higher. I looked at Addy again and tried to smile. My lips felt wobbly and unsure, but when she gazed back with friendship in her eyes, I knew for sure that whatever envelope she had planted in my backpack would not contain three hundred and fifteen dollars in small bills.

I breathed freely again, my sensation of free-fall interrupted. I had found my safety net—my friends. They'd never betrayed me at all, not even Addy. I could trust them.

As suddenly as I'd relaxed, I panicked again. The Doormat might not find money in my backpack, but there was something lurking in there as bad or worse—Brie's photographs! I seriously began to flop sweat at that point. The money I might have talked my way out of, but hard photographic evidence? No way.

Immediately after my realization, the vice principal withdrew an envelope from the back of my pack. Every worldly possession I had in that school was scattered on the floor before me, pawed over and scrutinized. In a few more moments, my dismal future would be on display as well.

I'd only just gotten my friends back. Now I'd lose them all over again.

"Well, well, well!" crowed Dermot, standing up. He started to rip the envelope open. I wondered how long it would be before he realized he held in his hands not the money he'd expected to find, but prints of me assaulting the bust of a U.S. president. "What have we here?" he said in a snide, nasty tone, even before he'd ripped open the flap.

"That's it!" Melinda cried. She shot me a look of triumph. It wasn't it, not at all, but I knew in a few more seconds she'd be crowing with glee.

"I believe here, Ms. Scott, that we have your . . ." The contents of the package fell out with a thump. "*DreemBoyz?*"

I blinked. *DreemBoyz?* Can we say *ewwww?* As if! This month's cover once again featured a huge photograph of the boy band S.W.A.K. Scotty, Wyatt, Antonio, and Kendrick flashed so many teeth to the camera that they looked like centerfold material for a female dentist. And *hello? Dreemboyz?* Spell check on aisle four!

Beside me now, Addy spoke up. "Are you sure it was stolen, Melinda? Maybe you stuck the envelope in your own bag by accident?" I gaped at Addy. She sounded so innocent and sweet and helpful you'd never know that behind her innocent exterior lurked someone with the deviousness of . . . well, of Melinda herself.

Melinda looked genuinely thrown by the discovery of the magazine. "I'm pretty sure I . . ." she said, instinctively bringing her bag around to check. Then she stopped as she realized what Addy had done to her. She shot us both a look of absolute hatred.

Disappointed though he was at not nailing me, Mr. Dermot sighed and put his hands on his hips. "Were you mistaken, Ms. Scott?"

It was too late now. With the slightest of gestures Melinda had led everyone to believe she would look through her own bag. Now everyone, from the Doormat to my friends to her own gaggle of onlookers, expected her to follow through. Despite a healthy coating of lipstick, her lips were practically white from how tightly she pressed them together while she flipped through her stuff. "Oh, look," she said, practically snarling. Honestly, if she'd been a dog, she'd have had foam flying from her mouth and Atticus Finch readying the shotgun in the background. "I must have put it in my own backpack. What a surprise."

The vice principal snatched the sealed envelope from her hands. Gio took the opportunity to kneel down on the floor and scoop my books back into my backpack.

"*DreemBoyz*?" I murmured to Addy. "Honestly."

"Hey, give me a break," she whispered back to me. "It was the only thing I could find on short notice."

"Three hundred, three-oh-five . . . three-fifteen," the Doormat murmured as he flipped through the bills. "This," he said to Melinda, wagging the bills back and forth, "is going to Mrs. Detweiler for immediate deposit, before it causes any more trouble."

"Oh, good," Melinda said, her voice cracking. She shot us a look that, had it been a harpoon, would have pierced concrete. "Addy, you're so *sweet* to help out. Thank you!"

Addy laughed and waved, her voice pure honey. "Anytime!" Under her breath, still smiling, she added, "You feeble fatheaded fartface."

The Hair Club girls who had been circling for blood slowly began to slink away. Melinda trudged behind them, thoroughly defeated. My own friends began to gather around me.

I should have been happy. One thing really nagged me though. I hated the fact that the Doormat was walking away without apologizing. I *deserved* that apology! "Vice Principal Dermot?" I said, trying to keep my tone polite and sweet.

"What?" he snapped, turning in his progress down the hall.

I held up my history textbook. "Illegal search and sei-zure. Fourth Amendment to the Constitution." I raised my eyebrow. "I'm sure my dad would love to have a little chat with you about it."

The Doormat stared, then shuddered. His shoulders hunched over as he scuttled away as quickly as his little legs could carry him. Hey, it wasn't an apology, but it surely made me happy.

I hugged them all, then. Every one of them—even Brie, the only one not in on the scheme. I hugged Gio last and longest. "You know," he said to me, "I don't know if I can date a girl who looks at *DreemBoyz*. Since when have you been a S.W.A.K. freak?"

"One word. Ew!" I said.

"Maybe she reads it for the articles," Addy teased.

"Is that my *DreemBoyz*?" I heard from the back.

"Oh, sorry, Dorie," said Addy. "I did borrow it from you. Don't be mean about S.W.A.K., anyone."

Brie snatched it from Gio's hands. "Nothing wrong with pictures of pretty, pretty boys."

While the others squabbled and bickered in a friendly way as we walked down the hall, I drew Addy ahead. "I'm sorry," she said instantly. "I'm so, so sorry."

"You know," I told her, "I'm sorry too, but let's save it for later. Be my friend now, okay?"

"Okay," she promised. After a second more, she added, "I wouldn't have drawn it out so much, but Melinda was so after your hide that she tried to recruit me right after I left you Friday. I had to see how far she planned to take things. You did tell me to pretend to be very, very angry with you."

"I didn't mean *that* much!" I protested, but I reached out and squeezed her hand to reassure her.

"And I'm sorry I told Brie about your . . . you know." She looked down at the floor. Behind us I heard Brie and Ray laughing about something or another. "That's what I'm sorriest about. I was so mad at you, though."

"I'm sorriest about that too. Hiding it for so long, I mean. I'm not the greatest friend."

"You can be."

I only had one question for her. "When did you know?"

"Oh, sweetie," she said simply. "Right from the start. I'm not a total doof!"

"Then why didn't you say anything?" I was dumbfounded at her answer. It was not what I had expected to hear. If it weren't for the fact that she seemed so matter-of-fact about it, I would almost have been embarrassed.

We stopped to let the others catch up. "You really needed to think you were special that way. I was just trying to protect you."

I wanted to hug her so badly right then, but she seemed a little shy. Later, I promised myself. "I'm truly sorry about you and Bart."

She rolled her eyes and her voice went back to a normal tone. "Don't be!" She laughed.

"I really do like your hair. You look so pretty."

"It's okay. I never thought I'd turn into one of those girls who'd end up spending all her allowance on *product.*"

Gio squeezed my shoulder as he joined us on my other side. It felt good to be touched. It felt even better to laugh. All this time I'd thought of myself as Vick the protector. Vick the fierce. And here I was, finally facing the fact I'd been protected by my friends to the very end. They didn't care how different or freakish I might be. I was one of them all the same. It felt strange.

It felt wonderful.

"What if I can't get back my seat in geometry?" Addy worried aloud.

"Let's not worry about the future yet," I told her. Together we opened the front doors and stepped outside while the others followed loudly behind. The sensation of spring sunshine on my face felt magical. "After all, the present's looking pretty darned good."

Amy Kaye

THE REAL DEAL

Focus on *THIS!*

Didn't want this book to end?

There's more waiting at **www.smoochya.com**:

Win FREE books and makeup!
Read excerpts from other books!
Chat with the authors!
Horoscopes!
Quizzes!

smooch Bringing you the books on everyone's lips!